Hiding Place

Hiding Place

Collin Wilcox

Random House: New York

With the deepest thanks,
this book is dedicated to

Kenneth Millar

Hiding Place

One

I unlocked my top right-hand desk drawer and grunted as I drew my revolver. I balanced the .38 in my hand, idly frowning at my "in" basket. The basket had been empty when I'd left to get a haircut an hour ago. Now two letters, a departmental memo, and a manila case folder lay in the gray metal tray.

I used the gun barrel to push the memo aside, revealing the folder's label. Recognizing the case, I sighed, surrendering to a Monday morning's moment of glum self-pity. Outside, the sky was cold and gray, threatening a day-long winter's rain. I'd just come off a sunny three-day weekend, after sixteen straight days of duty. And already my fellow officers were up to their departmental tricks.

Irritably I ignored the "in" basket, looking instead at the .38, held flat on my open palm. The gun needed cleaning. For more than a month, ever since I last fired it, I'd been meaning to clean the gun thoroughly, instead of haphazardly swabbing out the bore with powder solvent.

Years ago, when I'd first made inspector, I had faithfully cleaned the revolver once a week, every Friday. But the feel of the gun had been different then—different in my hand, different

1

on my hip. Years ago the metallic bulge beneath my coat had seemed my very special secret. Now the gun sometimes seemed merely a bulky nuisance.

I laid it in the open drawer. The drawer was stained with gun oil, even though I'd had the office for less than a year. Had the desk's previous owner kept his gun in the same drawer? I'd never know. The previous owner, Lieutenant Travis, had died in the men's room, of a heart attack. After almost thirty years of "meritorious duty serving the people of San Francisco," they'd found Travis propped against a urinal, dead.

No one had really mourned him. As he'd gotten older, Travis had started to believe his own press clippings.

The gun, I noticed, was scarred and worn-looking. Bright metal showed through the bluing; the walnut grips were chipped and scratched.

The departmental psychologist had once said that a cop's gun was his phallic wish-fulfillment. Cops, he'd said, fondled their guns instead of themselves. He'd been drunk at a Christmas party when he'd said it—sloppily, pugnaciously drunk. But no one would fight with him, and he'd finally passed out, snoring loudly, mouth wide open, his dentures clicking as he breathed. He'd been . . .

A knock sounded on my office door.

"Come in." I closed the drawer, turning the key.

Pete Friedman, my senior co-lieutenant, stood in the open doorway. As usual, his suit was rumpled, his collar wilted, his vest powdered with chronic cigar ash. His shirt bloused between his vest and his belly-bagged trousers. His collar was unbuttoned, his twisted tie loosened.

Smiling quizzically, he glanced amiably toward my "in" basket as he nodded a sly, knowing greeting. "I see you got the Wagner case." He eased his bulk into my visitor's chair, sighing deeply, settling himself elaborately. "No hard feelings, I hope. The captain decided to give you a shot at it, with my blessing."

"That case," I said slowly, "is three months old. Half the witnesses aren't even around."

2

"Four months old, actually. Don't worry about the witnesses, though. They weren't worth a damn."

"What am I supposed to do, read it and file it with my other sixty-two open cases?"

He shrugged indifferently, drawing a cigar from his vest pocket. "Use your own judgment. As far as I'm concerned, Wagner is just another dead hooker. She turned the wrong trick, and got herself strangled. Probably the John couldn't get an erection, so he strangled her instead. Or maybe it was one of those sadistic-masochistic tricks. That's very big now, I understand."

"And the John left town. And has never been traced. Right?"

"Now, now, don't get testy. You've got to expect these things, when you haven't been a lieutenant for even a year." He lit the cigar, shook the dead match once, and dropped it into my wastebasket, trailing a tiny plume of smoke. As I turned to stare pointedly at the paper-filled basket, I heard him saying, "When you're the senior homicide lieutenant—when I'm comfortably retired, that is—you'll have the privilege of sloughing off your unwanted cases on your fellow officer. Besides, maybe you'll get lucky with Wagner. A different approach, you know, can often do . . ."

My phone rang.

"Lieutenant Hastings."

"Just a minute, Lieutenant. I have Sergeant Markham for you." It was Communications.

A moment later Markham came on the line. His voice was metallic; he was calling on his radio. "We've got a homicide in Golden Gate Park, Lieutenant—a female Caucasian, about eighteen years of age. Apparently she's been dead since last night. She's been bludgeoned. She seems to be clean and well dressed. Her name is apparently June Towers, address 848 Twenty-fourth Avenue."

"Robbed?"

"Looks like it."

"Raped?"

"I don't think so."

3

"Anyone else on the scene with you?"

"Just me and Culligan. And the park patrolman who discovered the body."

I glanced at my watch; the time was 11:15 A.M. The date was January 17. June Towers was our first homicide of the new year. With last year's San Francisco homicides totaling more than a hundred, she was an overdue statistic.

"All right," I said into the phone, "I'll call the lab and the M.E. and the coroner. I'll be out in a half-hour. You'd better get reinforcements."

"I've already put in the call. A black-and-white car's just now arriving, in fact."

"Anything else to report?"

"No. Culligan's trying to line up possible witnesses, and the uniformed man is guarding the body. So far there isn't a crowd."

"Roger. I'll see you in a half-hour or so."

"Right."

I broke the connection and gave the necessary orders, instructing Canelli to get my car. Finally I swiveled to face Friedman.

"I was beginning to believe the mayor's oratory about how we're stamping out violent crime." He leaned laboriously forward, flicked his cigar ash into my wastebasket, then subsided, grunting. In the field—in action—Friedman could be surprisingly quick on his feet, especially taking cover. In the office, though, he seemed incapable of more than a portly, rolling waddle, propelling himself like an overweight banker from one chair to another, always seating himself with a long, grateful sigh.

I gestured to my "in" basket. "Wagner will have to wait."

"Obviously. Who's dead?"

"A teen-aged girl named June Towers. Well dressed. Lived in the Sunset, apparently. Robbed. Not raped." I unlocked my top desk drawer.

"I wonder why Markham bothered to call in. Since he's made acting sergeant, I'd expect him to be even more one-way than ever. Which is pretty one-way."

"Here—" I pushed an ashtray across the desk.

Flicking the ash without looking, and missing the tray, Friedman said, "Did you recommend Markham for sergeant?"

"No."

"I didn't either; I was for Culligan. Markham must've been entirely the captain's idea."

"Culligan's a good man, but he's got an ulcer," I said shortly. "He's a worrier. Besides, Markham's smart." I scanned the two letters and the memo, and returned them to the basket. "Markham's efficient too, and he doesn't get rattled."

"But you don't like him much."

"I wish he'd smile once in a while. But for that matter, I wish Culligan would smile once in a while." I holstered my gun.

"I could say the same about you, if you want the truth. The plain fact is, there really aren't many laughs in this business. It's . . ."

My phone rang.

"Lieutenant Hastings."

"Frank?" It was Ann.

"Yes."

"Are you busy?"

"Well, I . . ."

"I'll just be a minute. That's all I can talk, actually. I'm between classes. But I just wanted to tell you that Billy's spending the night with a classmate. So I wondered whether—" She let it go unfinished.

Glancing at Friedman, half turning away, I spoke into the phone. "Why don't I call you about five? Maybe we can go to a movie. I'm not sure, though. I'll have to see how things work out."

"Fair enough. I'll be home by four-thirty. 'Bye."

"Goodbye." As I hung up, I realized that I was avoiding Friedman's eye.

"Don't let me keep you from the year's first corpse," he said breezily. "I'll stay here and finish my cigar, if you don't mind. Sometimes I think better in your office than in mine."

"You'll probably set it on fire." I rose, taking my coat from the rack.

5

"Was that Ann Haywood? Your favorite grammar-school teacher?"

"Yes."

He nodded mock-solemnly. "If I were you, I think I'd marry her. You might not realize it, but your face actually softens when you talk to her. Or for that matter, when you talk *about* her. I'll bet you didn't know that."

"Listen, Pete, Canelli's probably . . ."

"How long have you known her?"

"Approximately a month, as a matter of fact. Not that it's really any of your . . ."

"You've smiled more this last month than you have during all of last year. Not only that, but my wife thinks you're perfect for each other. Did you know that?"

"This is beginning to sound more like a sorority house than a homicide bureau."

"Hmm—" Drawing on his cigar, he wagged his head elaborately, projecting a judicious approval. "Not a bad crack, considering that you're not really a comic type. Maybe it's Ann's softening influence."

"Shall I close my door? Or would you rather have it open?"

"Closed, please. Good luck."

Two

I braced myself as the car lurched around the corner. Canelli drove like he did everything else: earnestly but clumsily, constantly at odds with the job at hand. Yet, somehow, Canelli managed to blunder through, thanks to an incredible run of perpetual good luck. The entire homicide detail could be searching for a suspect while that same suspect was tapping Canelli on the shoulder, asking for a match. It was Friedman's theory that Canelli was lucky for all the wrong reasons: because he neither looked like a cop nor acted like a cop nor thought like a cop. Canelli was twenty-eight, weighed two hundred forty pounds, and usually looked as if he'd just gotten off an all-night bus. He never wore his haphazardly creased hat at the same angle, and he often needed a shave. His large brown eyes were round and wondering. His habitual expression was a thoughtful, half-perplexed frown. Canelli was the only cop I'd ever known who could actually get his feelings hurt.

"It can't be much farther, Lieutenant. Maybe a mile, at the most."

"You don't have to rush, Canelli. The lab crew is only ten minutes ahead of us."

7

"Right." He slowed the car, but still managed to throw us awkwardly around the next curve. The park was almost deserted; the sky was a grim winter's gray, still threatening rain. The tall trees were dark, featureless blobs of leaden green; the broad, sweeping lawns were lusterless. Yet yesterday the weather had been bright and warm: a perfect January day, cloudless and cheerful. Yesterday the park would have been crowded with cars, bikes, and hundreds of Sunday strollers— even a few hearty picnickers.

"I wonder how many murders've been committed in this park," Canelli was saying. "Hundreds, I bet. Maybe thousands."

"Maybe not. Don't forget, San Francisco didn't always have this kind of a homicide rate."

He nodded in thoughtful agreement. "You know, Lieutenant, I been an inspector for two years—just two years. But just in two years, the homicide rate's doubled. It's hard to believe. When I first made inspector, we were getting about forty murders a year."

"It's very simple, Canelli: it's the junkies. Just about two years ago the junkies started coming to town. If they aren't killing each other because of burn jobs, they're robbing to get enough money for the next fix. And a junkie with a gun is eventually a murderer."

"I was reading in the *Reader's Digest* that about seventy percent of all violent crime is connected to junk. Do you think that's right, Lieutenant?"

"Yes."

"Well, if it *is* right, then why don't the government just lean on places like Turkey, and make them cut out raising poppies? I mean, if we can send a man to the moon, then I don't see why we can't . . ."

"You're forgetting about the juice, Canelli. Heroin is big business. A lot of people have to be paid off to make it all work. If there're no more poppies, there're no more payoffs. A lot of people would have to switch from Cadillacs to Buicks. It's that simple."

"You really think so, Lieutenant? Honest?"

8

"Six months ago I had to go to New York. I had lunch with a precinct captain, up in Harlem. He was just retiring, so he didn't have to watch what he said. And he told me he could bust a dozen pushers that afternoon, carrying. But the next day they'd be right back on the street."

"Graft, eh?"

"It's not even as simple as graft. This captain said something that made me think. He said that like it or not, we're at war with the blacks—the ghetto blacks, anyhow. Maybe no one knows how the war started, or who's right, or how it'll end. It's like every other war: God's on both sides. But anyhow, this captain said that heroin is permitted in Harlem for one very simple reason: because it's just about the most effective weapon that the whites have against the blacks. He said that . . ."

Ahead, I saw the familiar, haphazard cluster of radio cars, cruisers, vans, and press cars.

"Jeez," Canelli was saying, bouncing the car off the curb as he pulled to a stop, "it really makes you think. I mean, that's like —like using poison gas, or something."

I swung open the door.

Immediately Kanter from the *Sentinel* and Ralston from the *Transcript* were beside me, one on either side. Kanter, on the morning paper, had lots of time. But Ralston, I knew, had a twelve-thirty deadline, just thirty minutes away.

"What's it look like, Lieutenant?" Ralston asked, walking so close that his shoulder jostled mine.

"Have you seen the body?" I asked him.

"Yes."

"Have you talked to Markham?"

"Yes. But—"

"Then you know more than I do."

He eyed me suspiciously. "No crap, Lieutenant?"

I smiled at him sardonically. "I wouldn't give you any crap, Ralston. Not after that piece you did on me a couple of weeks ago. The one about how the dog tore my pants while I was going after a suspect."

9

He was a tall, gaunt man with uneasy eyes, bad breath, and a wolfish, unpleasant grin.

"Sorry, Lieutenant. I couldn't resist it. I mean—candy-striped shorts."

"Just don't park near any fireplugs, Ralston."

"I was humanizing the policeman, Lieutenant. It's part of our new policy." But he couldn't keep his mouth straight. And out of the corner of my eye I saw Canelli's full lips twitching.

"I've got work to do," I said shortly. "As soon as I have something, I'll let you know. Now stand back."

The half-circle of detectives, lab men, and the coroner's crew parted silently as I stepped to the body.

She'd been dragged into a small, semi-concealed area in which dead branches and grass cuttings were piled, awaiting collection by the park's maintenance trucks. The area was surrounded on three sides by thick laurel bushes growing a foot above my head. She was on her back, feet primly together, hands along her sides. Her long dark hair lay upward from her head; she looked as if she were falling feet first through the air, hair streaming up as she fell. The murderer must have dragged her to the spot by her hair.

He'd have gotten bloody hands. Her hair was blood-matted; her forehead and ears and neck were caked almost black. Her face was oval, well shaped. Her brown eyes stared straight up; her mouth hung half open. Her teeth were white and even. She looked as if she might have swallowed her tongue.

She wore a hand-knit fisherman's sweater over an ordinary white shirt, open at the throat and cut like a man's. Her jeans were elaborately paisley-patched in the current teen-age fashion, bleached and spot-dyed, held by a silk scarf pulled through the belt loops. The scarf was knotted, the jeans buttoned. She wore beautifully made high-laced boots that could have cost fifty dollars. The boots were almost new.

Turning away, I studied the trail that her body had made through the park's dead leaves and twig-littered dirt. Two parallel lines of white tape led to a small grassy glade almost entirely surrounded by pine and eucalyptus trees. The glade was approximately a hundred feet from the spot where I stood, and would be almost completely invisible from both the nearby road and the sidewalk. Two patrolmen stood among the trees, on guard.

"What about a purse?" I asked Markham, standing beside me.

"Over in that clearing." He pointed. "She was killed over there."

Signaling for him to follow and for the lab crew and police photographers to continue their work, I began to pace slowly beside the tapes, my eyes on the ground. The murderer had made no effort to conceal his victim's trail; two long, wobbling grooves had been clearly scratched in the ground by the expensive boots.

Midway to the clearing I paused, pivoting, studying the terrain. The road was about fifty feet away, down a gentle, treeless slope. Assuming that she'd been murdered in the clearing just ahead and that she'd been dragged to the shelter of the laurel bushes, then the murderer and his victim would have been exposed to view from the road for approximately a hundred feet, the distance from the glade to the debris pile.

Either he'd killed her after dark, or he'd been very lucky. Or both.

I allowed my gaze to wander idly over the ground, surrendering myself to the whim of random thought, seeking some sense of how it could have happened. Sometime late yesterday the murderer had passed the spot where I now stood. He'd been dragging his victim toward the shelter of the laurel bushes. He'd had blood on his hands. Bending double over the body, panting, dragging her by the hair, he must have been terrified—looking wildly over his shoulder with each step.

Was he a madman?

Probably not. If he'd been a madman, he'd have raped her, or mutilated her, or arranged her body in some obscene pose, getting his kicks.

Was he a mugger—a hood, prowling the park's forest-like terrain, hunting a victim?

"Who found her?" I asked.

"A little guy named Lester Farley. Over there." Markham pointed to a black-and-white car. A figure was seated in the back, alone.

"Have you interrogated him?"

"Not really."

I ordered Canelli to question Lester Farley, then turned back to Markham. "What about a weapon?"

"No luck yet. But I haven't started a real search."

"What kind of a weapon does the M.E. think it was?"

"A pipe, probably. Or a heavy metal rod. Something about a half-inch in diameter, anyhow. Her skull's dented in. It required a lot of force, according to the M.E."

As we passed between the huge pine and eucalyptus trees circling the grassy clearing, Markham pointed to traces of blood on the grass, then to a separately taped-off purse lying less than a yard from the gleaming black boots of a patrolman. "There's her pocketbook. It's been photographed and printed, so you can handle it."

"Thanks." I deliberately flatted my voice. Markham was the man who would doubtless someday be my co-lieutenant. I wasn't looking forward to it.

I nodded to the patrolman and stooped to pick up the purse, holding it carefully in full view of the three men. It was actually a small rattan satchel, made in Hong Kong. Even the two catches were fashioned of wooden pegs and rattan loops. The purse had been lying open, presumably just as it had been found. Inside was the usual jumble of keys, Kleenex, and cosmetics. A red plastic wallet had apparently been thrust hastily into the satchel. The wallet had been left open. Random bits of paper protruded from the red plastic at odd angles. The section designed for currency was empty.

"Is this exactly the way you found it?" I asked.

"Yes."

"Did the lab print the card folder?"

"Yes." In his voice was a hint of irritation that he didn't bother to conceal. Markham didn't like to be pressed.

Withdrawing the fan of plastic folders, I found a driver's license, a library card, a BankAmericard, a Macy's charge card, and a student-body card from Alta High School—all made out to June Towers, age seventeen, a senior in Alta. In six months she'd have graduated.

I replaced the identity folder and emptied the wallet of everything else. I found a small color snapshot of a good-looking teen-age boy, a receipt for three records totaling $13.64, an address book covered in red watered silk and three slips of paper, each with someone's first name and phone number.

After copying her address, I returned everything to the billfold, leaving it all for the lab men. Turning to Markham, I said, "I'll talk to Lester Farley for a minute, then Canelli and I will start with her parents. You and Culligan stay here until you're sure you've got everything. Try to find the weapon. He probably threw it as far as he could, into some bushes. Give it plenty of time—two, three hours; if you have to, more. Use all the men you need; right now we haven't got anything else current. Make sure Ralston gets something for his paper, and take care of the radio and TV reporters. When the story's out, the chances are you'll have some witnesses showing up. I'll see you downtown about five, and we can compare notes."

"Are you sure you want me to spend a lot of time with a bunch of half-assed witnesses?" It was more than a question. It was a complaint—even a challenge.

At age thirty, good-looking and arrogantly self-confident, Markham had always reminded me of a too-handsome, too-ambitious Hollywood actor playing a badman in a "B" Western. Maybe it was the way he moved: slowly, smoothly, deliberately —as if each movement was carefully rehearsed. Or maybe it was his eyes: calm and cold—killer's eyes.

"This is a percentage business," I answered. "Talk to enough jerks and you'll eventually get something you can use. I'll see you about five." I held his eye for a last long moment, then turned away. He hadn't dropped his glance.

As I approached the black-and-white car, Canelli got out of the back seat, moving several paces away from the car, waiting for me. Lester Farley remained inside.

"Did you get anything from him?" I asked.

"Well," Canelli said slowly, "not much, I guess. But still—" He frowned thoughtfully, looking away, rubbing his chin. Watching him, I was thinking that Canelli would probably never master the rudiments of law-enforcement officialese. His reports read like high-school compositions laced with phrases from *Official Detective*.

I waited. Finally, refocusing his gaze and clearing his throat, he said, "Farley spends a lot of time in the park here. He's a walker, he says. He's unemployed and he lives with his mother, just about four blocks from here. He's been unemployed for three years, it turns out. But anyhow, the point is that he was here yesterday, too. Yesterday and today both. And he saw the victim yesterday. Right here." Canelli waved his hand vaguely.

I looked up at the secluded area where the body had been found, a hundred feet from the sidewalk. "He must be a cross-country walker. He couldn't have seen the body from either the sidewalk or the pathway."

"Yeah."

"What else?"

"Well, nothing else, really. Except that—" Again he frowned, struggling with the thought. "Except that he seems like kind of a kinky little guy. And you hear about these guys returning to the scene of the crime, and everything. So—" He shrugged.

"Do you have his address?"

"Yessir. And his mother's name. He has identification, too."

"All right. Get him out here."

Canelli stepped to the car, opening the door, beckoning. A slight, anxious-looking man emerged, blinking, and hesitantly approached me. He looked to be in his early forties. Everything about him was pale and frail-looking: sallow complexion, faded blue eyes behind bookkeeper's glasses, thinning blond hair, a pursed cupid's mouth. He wore a tan jacket and dark brown slacks. His clothing was neat and clean, his shoes shined. He was a nondescript, harmless-looking little man.

I introduced myself and asked him to repeat his account of finding the body. Telling the story, talking in a low, precise mon-

14

otone, he seemed strangely unshaken by his recent encounter with violent death.

"I was out for a morning walk," he said primly, "and I saw her lying there. At first I just saw her feet. Then, when I got closer, I saw—all of her." Involuntarily his glance strayed up the gentle slope to the cluster of men surrounding the body. Two stretcher bearers were approaching the group. Soon the body would be moved.

"What time was it that you discovered the body?"

"It was about ten o'clock."

I gestured up the slope, saying, "To have seen her feet in that area where she was found, screened on three sides by bushes, you'd've had to've been walking across the grass."

"Yes."

I looked down at his shoes. They were actually high-laced hiking boots, moccasin-toed.

"The grass would've been wet. It's still a little wet."

He nodded. "Yes, it was wet. But I walk a lot. I don't work. And I like to exercise. So I walk."

I eyed him silently for a moment, looking him over, taking my time. His reaction was a slightly puzzled, puckered frown. He didn't squirm under my scrutiny.

"You were here yesterday, too," I said finally.

"Yes."

"You saw the victim then, too."

"Yes, I did."

"What time was that, Mr. Farley?"

"It was about four-thirty in the afternoon, I'd say."

"What was the victim doing when you saw her?"

He shrugged. "She was just standing there." He pointed to a point perhaps twenty feet beyond my car. "She was standing by the popcorn wagon."

"Was she buying popcorn?"

"No. She was just standing there."

"How'd you happen to notice her? Had you ever seen her before?"

He shook his head slowly. He stole another glance up at the

murder scene. The official group was parting, making way for the stretcher bearers.

"Did you see anyone else yesterday that you recognized?"

"No, I'm afraid not."

"What about the popcorn man? Had you seen him before?"

"Well, yes. But I thought you meant—" He fluttered a narrow, delicate hand, letting the sentence go unfinished.

"If we were to collect a group of people—random people—do you think you could pick out one or two who'd been in this area yesterday?"

He moistened his lips, frowning, blinking. "I—I'm not sure what you mean."

"Well," I said slowly, consciously projecting an air of deliberate patience, "you were able to identify the murder victim as having been here yesterday. I'd think you could do the same for others." I paused, watching him carefully. "Or was there something special about the girl that made you remember her?"

Startled, he looked at me quickly. "No," he answered. "There was nothing—nothing at all. I just—just recognized her, that's all."

I stared at him for a last long, silent moment, then extended my hand. His grip was limp. "Thanks a lot, Mr. Farley. You've been a big help. We'll want to get a statement from you. So be sure and keep yourself available."

"Yes. Thank you. I will." He nodded to both of us, smiled nervously, and began walking away.

I gestured to Culligan, unobtrusively standing by. "Follow him," I ordered. "Check him out."

"Right."

I watched them out of sight: the slim, skittish subject and the tall, gangling detective moving stolidly along the sidewalk.

"I don't think Culligan is much of a walker," Canelli said.

Shrugging, I turned to my car. "It was him or you, Canelli. Look at it that way. Come on. We're going to the victim's house."

Three

"Nice place," Canelli commented as we pulled to the curb in front of June Towers' house. "Forty, forty-five thousand, at least."

"You're probably right."

"I don't live so far from here," he volunteered. "But not in any forty-thousand-dollar house. Every block you get away from the park, the value goes down."

I hesitated, then decided to ask, "How is it you still live with your parents, Canelli?"

He looked thoughtful for a moment, rubbing his chin. Finally: "I guess it's because of Gracie. My girl friend. I guess you never met her." He looked at me. "Have you?"

"No."

"I didn't think so."

I waited. I realized that I was playing games with myself, deliberately delaying the moment when I'd have to tell the girl's parents that their daughter was dead.

"See," Canelli was saying, "Gracie and me, we been going together for about six years—ever since I got out of the navy, almost, and joined the force. And it seems like every year we

17

think we're going to get married, but then we never do. So that's why."

I smiled to myself, thinking of Friedman's squad-room fun commenting on Canelli's syntax.

"That's why you still live with your folks, you mean."

He nodded. Taking his cue from me, he was simply sitting behind the wheel, looking straight ahead. Then I saw him frown slightly. I recognized the expression. He was framing a difficult question.

"How long has it been since you been, ah, not married, Lieutenant?"

"Almost ten years," I answered shortly. "Too long."

"Yeah, I see what you mean. That's a long time, all right." Again he hesitated before deciding to say, "I bet it must seem kind of, ah, funny, having your family back East. Your kids, I mean."

I put my hand on the door handle. "I don't recommend divorce, Canelli. You're doing the right thing. Long courtships might be out of fashion, but they're a hell of a lot better than short marriages." I swung the door open. "I'll go talk to the parents. I want you to call in to Lieutenant Friedman. Tell him that I'd like to have him locate that popcorn vendor. And tell him that I'll fill him in when I know a little more. After you've done that, come inside." I jerked my chin toward the house. "Clear?"

"Yessir." He reached for the mike.

On the first peal of the chimes the door opened. A woman in her late thirties stood in the doorway. Seeing me, her eyes instantly glazed with the disbelief of someone facing certain disaster. Her body was rigid, braced against my first words. She was a glossy blonde, beauty-shop-beautiful.

Her eyes first searched my face, then fled to the car behind me. "Are you fr—fr—" Momentarily she stuttered. "From the police?"

"Yes, Mrs. Towers. I'm Lieutenant Hastings." I took off my hat. "May I come in?"

Her painfully arched body suddenly went slack. She sagged

18

against the doorframe, her hands clasped knuckle-white at her waist. Her lips began to twitch.

"What is it?" she whispered. "What's happened? Is June—" She began to shake her carefully coiffed head in a dull, defeated arc. Finally, with great effort, she looked at me directly, mutely imploring me not to tell her what she knew I'd come to say.

"I'm afraid June is dead, Mrs. Towers. She—they found her in the park about an hour ago. Just a few blocks from here."

She was still shaking her head slowly from side to side. Somehow she reminded me of a dazed, stubborn child refusing to eat her dinner. Her hands were clasped cruelly, pressed tightly into the pale-beige cashmere of her sweater just below her breasts.

Through stiffened lips she said, "My name isn't Towers. It's Grant—Ellen Grant."

"Why don't we go inside, Mrs. Grant? We can sit down. You can . . ."

A man stood behind her. His dark, thick hair was finger-combed, his jowls unshaven. In his early forties, broad and beefy, he was glaring at me with the suspicious, belligerent look of a barroom stud who suspects that someone has insulted his wife.

As the man was about to speak, Ellen Grant suddenly wheeled, blindly striking his shoulder with hers as she blundered past him into the house.

I introduced myself to Randall Grant and briefly explained what had happened. As I was talking, Canelli joined us, nodding to me, signifying that he'd gotten through to Friedman. Then the three of us silently entered the ornate living room, already touched by the hush of violent death.

Ellen Grant sat hunched against the arm of a silk-brocaded easy chair. She was sobbing painfully, her body racked with dry, gasping spasms. Her eye make-up had dissolved into dark, grotesque smears, distorting the contours of her face, suggesting a surrealistic caricature of gross, ugly grief. Her hands hung limply across the silken arm of the chair. Some of her mascara-stained tears had fallen on the off-white brocade. Silently Canelli put a handkerchief in her hand, then sat down on a sofa that matched the chair. In his rumpled blue suit, with his misshapen hat beside him on the sofa, Canelli looked as incongruous as ever. His broad face was lightly glazed with perspiration. Whenever Canelli was forced to endure someone else's grief, he perspired.

Grant's expression was still faintly belligerent as he stood before a black onyx fireplace, looking down at his wife. He made no move to touch her; he hadn't spoken to her directly. He was dressed casually in a knit shirt, wide-striped trousers, and soft leather shoes. Except for his dark, unshaven jowls, he looked as if he were ready for a round of country-club golf. His face was handsome but heavily cast: humorless, stolid, sullen. The muscles of his arms were thick and firm, but his neck was beginning to sag. The knit shirt revealed a bulge at the waist.

Blowing her nose in Canelli's handkerchief, the woman choked, then gasped, "I knew it. I knew she'd been killed. It— it's the only thing it could've been. The only thing." Suddenly she twisted toward her husband. "I *told* you she wouldn't stay out all night."

Deliberately pitching my voice to a quiet note, I said, "Do you have a picture of your daughter, Mrs. Grant? We'd like to borrow it."

The man swung abruptly away from the fireplace. "I'll get you one."

"Don't take the one on my dresser," she said petulantly. "Take her yearbook picture."

"I know which one to take." His voice was abrupt, his dark brows gathered in an irritable frown. He was already halfway across the room, plainly anxious to be free from the sight of his sobbing wife. I caught Canelli's eye, moving my head toward the departing man. Nodding, Canelli rose. He would detain Randall Grant in another part of the house and question him separately.

I took out my notebook and ballpoint pen, saying, "I realize this is a bad time for you, Mrs. Grant. But there're some questions I've got to ask you, some information that we need. The sooner we get it, the sooner we can find out who killed your daughter. Do you understand?"

20

"Y—yes." She blew her nose again, daubed at her smeared eyes, and drew a long, shaky sigh. "Wh—what d'you want to know?"

"First, when was the last time you saw her? What time was it, and where did she say she was going?"

"It—it was about three o'clock yesterday. Sunday. She said she was going for a drive. She said she'd probably be back in a few hours."

"What kind of a car was she driving?"

"It—it's a Volkswagen. Green."

"A bug?"

She nodded, again drawing a deep, unsteady breath. She was shakily gaining control of herself. It was my chance to get the information I needed, then get out—before a second rush of grief overcame her. For the moment she was partially anesthetized by shock. I could clearly recognize the signs: the slightly unfocused eyes, the short, shallow breathing, the slack, almost listless droop of arms and shoulders.

"Was the car registered to you, Mrs. Grant?"

"Yes. But it was really my daughter's. We—I—gave it to her last summer."

"She didn't mention any specific destination—anything she wanted to do, anyone she wanted to see? She was just going out for a drive?"

"Y—yes."

"Was she upset when she left?"

At the question, her eyes strayed aside, involuntarily seeking the rear of the house where her husband had gone. Finally, licking at her lips, Ellen Grant said, "She wasn't upset. Not really. I mean—" She hesitated, again glancing aside. Now her expression was bitter, baleful. "My husband and I, we—" She paused. Suddenly her lips were curling, as if she'd just pronounced an obscenity. "We were fighting. We—we're just about to get a divorce. We've been talking about it for weeks now—months. So yesterday we were fighting, and I told him to—to leave. Just leave. So then June, she—" The woman's voice suddenly caught. But, doggedly, she continued: "She walked into the living room, from the back of the house. She—she said that she was sick of hearing us fight and that she was going for a drive. Anything, just to get out. And that—" She gulped, suddenly pressing the handkerchief to her nose. "And that's the—the last I saw of her."

"Mr. Grant isn't—wasn't—June's father."

"No."

"Is her father in the city?"

Her voice was sharp as she said, "I don't know where he is. I married him when I was nineteen, because I had to. Six months later he disappeared. I never saw him again—never heard from him or got a penny from him."

"You haven't seen the girl's father, or been in contact with him, for approximately sixteen years, then. Is that right?"

"Th—that's right. I heard *about* him a couple of years ago. But that's all."

"What'd you hear about him?"

"That he was a bum," she said bitterly. "Which is what he always was, I guess. In his whole life he never did anything but common labor. But—" Her voice was softer as she said, "But I was too young, then, to know the difference. All I knew was that"—she drew a deep, unsteady breath—"that every time he touched me, I liked it. And now he—he won't even know she's dead."

"Can you give me any idea why she might've been killed, Mrs. Grant? Did she have any enemies?"

She looked as if I'd suddenly slapped her. "Everyone liked June," she whispered fiercely. "June was a good girl. A *good* girl."

I shook my head gravely. "Did she have any special friends?"

"She had lots of friends. *Lots* of them."

"Any boyfriends?"

"Yes. Kent Miller. They go to the same school. He lives just a few blocks from here. On Balboa."

"She just has the one boyfriend, you mean. They go steady."

"Yes. June didn't—play around, play off one boy against the other. She wasn't like that. She was—" Her voice caught. She was daubing at her eyes, sniffling. My time was running out. The

22

shock was wearing off; all her grief and pain and guilty memories were rushing back, suffocating her.

"For now," I said, rising to my feet, "I've just got one last question. I'd like to know whether your daughter was carrying any money in her purse."

"I—I suppose she had some. She always did. But she never got a lot of money. Not like some kids. I—I gave her five dollars a week. Period. For a—a long time June worked. Even though she always had enough money, she worked. Th—that's the way she was."

"So you would say," I persisted, "that she probably had, say, five dollars in her purse."

She nodded mutely.

I laid my card on the cocktail table. "I'll be in touch with you, Mrs. Grant. In the meantime, if you need anything from us— or if you have any information for us—call me at this number."

She was staring at the black onyx fireplace, oblivious of me. Slowly moving her head from side to side with an uncertain, almost querulous movement, eyes utterly empty and voice pitched to a low, disembodied note, she began to speak. "I waited on tables and hustled drinks to raise her. I even hustled men, when there wasn't anything else I could do. I finally married a man with money. He was thirty years older than me, and I couldn't stand to have him touch me. He died, and I did it again—the same thing. It—it gets easier, marrying for money. This is my fourth marriage, and except for that first time—with Towers—there's never been a minute when I even thought I was in love. I—I forgot how to laugh. And all the time I used to tell myself that it was all for her—for June. But I never really believed it, and neither did she. I—"

Suddenly she was doubled over, arms across her stomach, sobbing. I stood looking down at her for a moment, then decided to leave. Canelli was waiting for me in the open entryway. Randall Grant stood beside him, looking at his wife indifferently.

I made arrangements for Grant to identify the girl, then stepped outside, gesturing for Canelli to follow.

23

"Did you find out anything?" I asked.

"Not much. He's a big fat pain in the neck, if you ask me." "They're getting divorced. That's why they seem so strange." He snorted.

I said, "I want you to go back inside. See if you can get the license number of the car the girl was driving—a green VW. Get it on the air. Make sure they don't handle it as a routine stolen car, and make sure the lab'll run a fingerprint check on it if they find it. Then I want you to search through the girl's effects, thoroughly. The motive was probably robbery, but it's too early to tell. Find out everything you can about her. Try the neighbors. Everything. When you've finished, call for a radio car and take the stepfather to the morgue for identification. Unless there's something urgent, plan on being at the office at four-thirty or five. By that time the afternoon papers will be out and Markham'll probably have something from the scene. We might even have her car, if we're lucky."

"Right. What're you going to do, Lieutenant?"

"I'm going to interview the girl's boyfriend, and spend a couple of hours following my nose."

I realized that I didn't have Kent Miller's address. I debated for a moment returning to the house, but decided against it. Suddenly I was hungry. I'd stop for a drive-in hamburger and get the address from a phone book.

Four

The Miller house was comfortably middle-class, but smaller than the Grants'. Confirming Canelli's theory, the Millers' neighborhood was a block farther from the park than the Grants'. The lots were narrower, the lawns scruffier, the windows less elaborately draped.

As I rang the bell I glanced at my watch. The time was just two-thirty. Perhaps Kent Miller wouldn't be home from . . .

The door was opened by a slim, blond boy wearing boots, Levis, a sweatshirt, and a Mexican serape. I'd already seen his likeness in the snapshot June Towers had carried in her purse. He wore his hair earlobe-long, carefully combed. His features were regular, his brown eyes steady. He looked clean and alert as he smiled at me, then began to frown. Like the girl's mother, Kent Miller had already half guessed my identity.

As I broke the news I watched him intently. His first reaction was a deepening frown and a slow, numbed shaking of the head.

"Jesus," he mumbled. "June, too. Jesus."

"What'd you mean, 'too'?"

"Wh—what?" His expression was blank, baffled.

"You said 'June, too.' Did you mean that there was someone else—someone besides June?"

"I—I don't know what you mean."

I hesitated, carefully framing the question. "Do you mean to imply," I said slowly, "that others have died besides June Towers—that her death might be part of a pattern?"

"N—no. I just meant that—" He broke off, blinking, spreading his hands in a gesture that somehow reflected both the helplessness of childhood and the baffled frustration of the adult. "I j—just meant that everyone's getting ripped off. That's all I meant."

"Do you know anyone else who's been murdered?"

"Well, not—" He licked at his lips. "Not myself. Not personally. But Jesus, who'd want to kill June? She's—" Suddenly his eyes widened, his hands clenched involuntarily. Mouth open, he was staring past me as if he'd just glimpsed something strange and shocking.

He knew something—suspected something.

But I mustn't press him too hard, frighten him off. It was a delicate moment—possibly a decisive moment.

"Can we go inside?" I asked quietly. "I'd like to ask you some questions. You might be able to help us more than you realize."

Without waiting for his reply, I walked past him into the living room. It was an ostentatiously furnished room, crowded with adult toys.

"Are your parents home?" I sat down, gesturing him to a seat across from me.

For a moment, sinking into an imitation black leather chair, he didn't reply. He was still preoccupied—still stunned.

Finally he mumbled, "No, neither one of them are home. They won't be home till six. They—" He drew a deep, unsteady sigh. "They both work."

"That must be tough on you. With nobody here when you come home from school." It was a neutral, bland remark, meant to put him at ease—and to give myself a moment to think. In the absence of his parents, I must be careful not to

26

question him too closely. If he became a suspect, his lawyer could claim that I'd violated his civil rights by entering the premises without parental permission.

He didn't reply. But now, slowly, he was focusing on me. For a long moment I simply looked at him, searching for some small hint of guilt. Immediately he dropped his eyes, shifting uncertainly in his chair.

"I suppose," I said, "that you knew June was missing."

"Y—yes. Her folks called me last night. They wanted to know if I'd seen her."

"What time last night?"

"About—" He gulped. "About nine, I guess. Maybe nine-thirty."

"That's the first you knew of her disappearance?"

"Yes."

"Did you see her yesterday?"

"No. I—I talked to her on the phone, but I didn't see her."

"What time was it that you talked to her?"

"About—" He hesitated, glancing at me with a round-eyed expression of almost guileless apprehension. "About three o'clock, I guess it was. She said that her folks were fighting, and she was sick of it. She was splitting. She wanted to know if I'd come with her."

"You say 'splitting.' What'd you mean, exactly?"

He shrugged. "I mean that she was just—just going for a drive. Out. I don't know."

"How did she seem? Disturbed? Depressed?"

"Not depressed. Just bugged. She just wanted to"—he threw out one impatient hand in the typical gesture of the teen-ager searching for a word—"to split," he said finally.

"Why didn't you want to go with her?"

"Because I—" He paused. "I was working on my bike."

"A motorcycle?"

He nodded.

I returned his nod, absently fingering the crease in my trousers. I'd been trying to form some opinion of Kent Miller—get some feeling of his strength and his weakness, his doubts and his fears. So far, I hadn't succeeded. Like many teen-agers in trouble, he seemed simply to freeze—registering nothing, expressing nothing. His voice was uninflected, his gaze wary but unrevealing. He wasn't hostile, but neither was he friendly. He wasn't a delinquent type, and he certainly wasn't the standard version of the street-corner cop hater.

Yet something had caused the eye-widened, fist-clenched spasm of momentary apprehension. Was it guilt?

I didn't know. It could have been a sudden, overwhelming sensation of loss.

Was it guilt?

Could he have killed her?

Even at the wayward thought, I felt a fleeting sense of uneasiness. According to the law, it is at the time an officer first entertains a suspicion of guilt that he must advise the subject of his constitutional rights.

He was unsteadily lighting a cigarette, exhaling the smoke in a ragged plume.

"What kind of a motorcycle do you have?" I tried to make it a neutral question, reflecting no more than a casual interest.

"It's a Honda. A 350."

"Have you had it long?"

"About—about six months, I guess. Since summer."

Still casual, I smiled at him. "Did you get your motorcycle fixed yesterday?"

"Yes."

"Were you riding it yesterday?"

Cigarette half raised, he hesitated, watching me warily. "Yes," he answered slowly, still with the cigarette poised. "Yes, I rode it."

The moment had come. Either I pressed him, or I backed off. Suddenly my position seemed precarious. I was interrogating a teen-aged subject, possibly a suspect, without having given him his rights. I didn't have his parents' permission to enter the premises.

I'd disciplined subordinates for less.

I smiled, settling back in my chair, glancing at my watch. "I

28

don't have much time, Kent. I realize that you're upset—that talking about June doesn't help. But it's important, you know, that we get all the information we can as soon as we can get it."

"Sure. I understand." He waved the cigarette in a wobbly arc that was meant to convey a sense of unconcern. The gesture reminded me of a kid in high-school dramatics, unconvincingly playing drawing-room comedy.

"Can you think of anyone who would want to harm her?"

"No—no one." His voice had slipped into momentary falsetto.

"Had she ever had any trouble with boys? I mean, had she thrown anyone over recently—kissed anyone off?"

He shook his head, blinking now. "No. We—we've been tight for almost a year, June and me. We—" Suddenly tears were shining in his eyes. He was coming apart; my time was running out.

"You can't think of any reason why she might've been killed, then?" I said quietly. "None at all?"

He first shook his head, then shrugged. As he looked down into the ashtray, stubbing out his cigarette, a single tear streaked his cheek.

"Answer me, Kent," I said.

"No, I—" He gulped. "I—I can't think of anything. Nothing. June, she was cool. She didn't hassle. She just—" He didn't finish it. He sat with head lowered, grinding the dead cigarette into the ashtray.

"She wasn't involved with drugs, was she?"

Startled, he raised his head. "Wh—why do you—" He licked at his lips, staring at me.

"I'm asking," I said softly, "because I want to determine whether she might've had a drug habit that would've brought her into contact with underworld types—and that might've involved her carrying large sums of money. I'm not going to go through her room looking for a few marijuana flakes. That's not the purpose of the question. Do you understand?"

Plainly relieved, he nodded. Then he shook his head. "No,"

he answered, "June wasn't involved in anything heavy like that. Never." As he said it, he shook his head decisively.

"Good." I picked up my hat and got to my feet. "Well, I've got to be going." I pitched my voice to a brisk, friendly note. "I imagine," I said, walking into the hallway, "that it'll turn out to be a mugger—maybe a junkie, too strung out to know what he was doing. As soon as we find out anything, we'll be in contact with you. Meanwhile"—I handed him my card—"if you think of anything that might help us, please give me a call."

He looked down at the card, hesitated, then gingerly took it, holding it awkwardly between thumb and forefinger.

"And of course," I said casually, "we'll want you to come downtown to give us a formal statement."

"D—downtown? T—to police headquarters?" He seemed unable to comprehend it.

"In a day or so. There's no hurry. Meanwhile, thanks again. And if there's anything I can do—anything at all—please let me know." I turned the doorknob, and left him staring at my business card.

Five

I found a drugstore and called the office, asking for Pete Friedman.

"Canelli," he said dryly, "has just arrived. By luck, probably, he discovered something that will doubtless break the June Towers case wide open."

"What the hell's he doing down there? I told him to get some background information on the girl. Out here, in her neighborhood."

"I'll let him tell you. He'll naturally want to build the suspense. He's been loitering around outside my office like a pubescent girl waiting for the phone to ring. Right now—right this very minute—he's staring at me with those large, moist brown eyes. Which is one of the reasons that I've never liked these goddamn glass partitions."

"Anything from Markham?"

"He hasn't got much from the murder scene, but I think I've got a line on the popcorn vendor. I'll have him brought in. The Lester Farley tail just called—completely pooped. It seems that Farley's a walker. That's all, just a walker."

"Don't be too sure. At the moment he might be our best

prospect. He was one of the last ones to see her alive, and the first one to see her dead. That could be a lot more than coincidence."

"Sounds reasonable. He could've . . . Oh, oh. Wait a minute." The line clicked dead. Then: "They picked up her car, Frank. Just about a mile from the scene, in the park. I'm sending a man out to make sure they tow it into the lab."

"Good. Let me talk to Canelli. I'll see you at four-thirty or five."

"Roger." I heard him calling to Canelli, telling him to take my call in the squad room.

"Hello?" It was Canelli's voice.

"I hear you've got something."

"Oh, hello, Lieutenant. Yeah, I think I do. See, I went through her room, like you said, but after about fifteen minutes or so I hadn't found anything. I mean, I hadn't found anything that *meant* anything. No diaries, or letters, or anything. She was probably one of those kids who carried everything in her purse. So, anyhow—" He paused for breath. "So anyhow, after about fifteen minutes I was sitting on her bed, just looking around. And I though that what the hell, I should look for some grass, or drugs, or something—an envelope, say, taped somewhere. So I took out all her drawers and looked on the bottoms and the backs. But that didn't . . ."

"Canelli. Please. I don't need a blow-by-blow. Just tell me what you found."

"Oh. Sorry, Lieutenant. Well, I was just getting to the point. Which is that as a last resort, I looked up under the bed. And I almost missed it, because it was a brown envelope, the same color as the bed frame, Scotch-taped up there. And guess what I found."

I sighed. "I give up, Canelli. What'd you find?"

"I found three hundred and twenty-seven dollars. In cash. And that's why, see, that I thought I should come downtown, to turn the money in. I mean, I don't like to carry that much around."

"Why? Are you afraid you might get robbed?"

"What?" I could visualize him frowning, perplexed.

"Never mind. Tell me how her parents reacted."

"Well, they were pretty surprised. Especially her mother. She seemed to think I planted the money, or something."

"Did she try to account for it?"

"She said that up to a few months ago the girl used to work for a family named Cross, which lives just a couple of blocks from them. I mean, June used to baby-sit the Cross kid, mostly. And sometimes she'd fix dinner. Things like that."

"How much did she earn?"

"Twenty a week, average."

"Did she spend it all?"

"Her mother thinks so. And looking at the victim's clothes closet, I can believe it. Her mother, see, says that the victim bought her own clothes when she was working for the Crosses."

"And she hasn't worked for a few months you say."

"Right."

"Do you have the Crosses' address?"

"No, but I can get it out of my desk. Why?"

"Because," I said patiently, "I think I'd like to talk with them. We need all the information we can get on the victim, especially about her finances, as it turns out."

"Oh. Right. Just a minute." I heard him clumping across the squad room, then clumping back. "It's Walter Cross, Lieutenant, at 761 Twenty-sixth Avenue."

"Right. Now listen, Canelli—this money puts a different light on things, obviously. She sure as hell didn't save three hundred dollars on twenty dollars a week—not if she bought clothes. And even if she *did* save it, she'd have the money in the bank, not under the bed."

"I know it, Lieutenant. That's why, when I first saw it, I said to myself the money was probably hot. I figure that . . ."

"I want you to get back out here," I interrupted, "and try to make contact with some of the victim's friends. Try the neighbors, too. But be cool. Tell them that you heard June Towers had a lot of money, and ask them about it. Check on her spending habits, too. But don't admit that we have any specific suspicions."

"Right."

"If she kept three hundred dollars under the mattress," I said, "she could've been carrying a wad in her purse. That might be our motive. If so, it implies premeditation. Someone might've had prior knowledge that she had money on her. Which would mean that we aren't looking for a random mugger. It could be an entirely new ball game."

"I was just thinking the same . . ."

"I want you to be careful about suggesting to the parents, though, that the money might be hot. Just say that you're puzzled. Clear?"

"Yessir."

"All right. I'll check with the Crosses and see where that gets me. I'll see you downtown about four-thirty. Good luck."

"Thanks, Lieutenant. You, too."

"Thanks, Canelli. You might not need the luck, but I do."

Six

I parked across the street from the Cross residence, and for a moment simply sat in the car studying the house and the front yard. It was a large two-story house, probably less than twenty years old, obviously expensive. The front garden was beautifully planted, doubtless by a professional. Yet the house had an empty quality, as if its owners were away. A newspaper and several circulars littered the front porch.

As I walked toward the door, I looked up and down the block, watching the children play, listening to their laughter. It was a reassuring sound: the carefree libretto of the American middle class. Its cadence and timbre differed from the ghetto's. Its rhythms were lighter, less robust, less violent. Suddenly I realized that I was in my own territory. I felt safe. I was walking easily, muscles relaxed. Was it because I could recognize the same subtle rhythms that had accented my own childhood? Or was it because in the ghetto I was the enemy? Did the ghetto-sounds, like the jungle-sounds, change when an alien animal came close?

I rang the bell, waited, then rang again. I was about to turn away when the door opened. I was facing a man of about my own age, about my own height. He weighed a little less, probably about a hundred eighty. He wore his dark hair modishly long. He was dressed in khaki trousers, an old red sweater, and loafers. His beard was a day old. He blinked at the light as if he'd been inside too long. And, at three o'clock, alcohol was plain on his breath.

"Mr. Cross?"

"Yes." He was frowning, ready to deny whatever pitch I'd come to make. When I identified myself, showing him the shield, I saw a shadow shift behind his eyes. Was it the small shock that most citizens register when confronted by an unexpected badge? Or was it fear?

I asked to go inside, and after a brief hesitation he stood back, gesturing me past, closing the door. As I was sitting down, a name registered: Mrs. Walter Cross, residing in the Sunset District.

Several months ago she'd been a suicide. Accounting, doubtless, for the shadow-shift behind the eyes.

As quickly as I could, I stated my business, apologizing for the intrusion. His reaction was subdued, almost indifferent. He mumbled that he was very sorry about June—that she was a nice girl. Then he simply sat slumped in his chair. He was a handsome man, with moody eyes and a petulant, self-indulgent mouth. Even sitting down, the lines of his body suggested a certain overprivileged elegance. He looked like a successful advertising executive relaxing in his gardening clothes on a Sunday afternoon.

Except that it was Monday, and he had liquor on his breath. And the richly furnished house smelled stale and unused. Dirty dishes were everywhere: on the mantel, the bookcase, even the floor. On the side table I could see a coffee cup with green and white fungus growing in the bottom.

With an almost visible effort he focused his uncertain gaze on me. Anticipating my unspoken question, he said abruptly, "I don't go out much. Almost never, in fact. My wife—died, six months ago. And three months after that, her daughter—left. So—" His voice trailed off into a kind of exhausted silence. He

36

began gnawing at his lips as he stared down at the floor between his feet.

"I remember about your wife. Barbiturate overdose, wasn't it?" I pitched my voice to a neutral, professional note. After six months, sympathy wouldn't help him.

"It was barbiturates and liquor, I'm afraid. She—she drank a lot, the last year. And she began threatening suicide. Then she tried it, a couple of times—after giving me warning. Finally"— he choked, then cleared his throat—"finally she made it. I—I should have taken it more seriously when she first threatened. I know that now," he said, shaking his head in a dull, lifeless movement of self-pitying defeat.

To change the subject, I said, "Did you say your daughter left?"

"Not *my* daughter, Lieutenant. *Her* daughter. By a previous marriage." As he said it, his voice was edged with bitterness. "Katherine—my wife—was married before."

Still speaking in a flat, official monotone, I said, "How old was the daughter?"

"Seven."

"It would make sense, then, for her to go with her father."

His head bobbed loosely in a slack, long-suffering movement of impatient agreement. "The point is, Lieutenant, that she didn't *go* with the father, who happens to be a drunk—and who, incidentally, regularly beat Katherine. The girl's with her grandparents. After Katherine's death her parents wanted the little girl. They *had* to have her."

"Did you get a lawyer?"

He shook his head regretfully. "That's what I should've done. Just like I should've taken Katherine's suicide threats more seriously. But—" Very deliberately he stretched far back in the easy chair. He seemed to move with extreme care, as if any sudden movement would tip him beyond some delicate, desperate balance. With feet stretched far out, eyes closed, limp hands resting on either arm of the chair, he spoke in a very low voice. "Some people, you know, commit the most terrible sins imaginable, with the clearest, most untroubled consciences.

Katherine's parents, for instance, merely convinced themselves that they were acting in the best interests of their granddaughter. The rest—" He lifted one hand, then let it fall back. "The rest was easy."

"If I were you, Mr. Cross, I'd get out of here. Do you work?"

His head was resting against the back of the chair, neck arched, eyes still closed. I saw his expressive, well-shaped mouth stir in a small, rueful smile.

"I'm an interior decorator, Lieutenant. I was a fairly good, fairly successful one when Katherine and I met. She was a client of mine, in fact. She'd just gotten divorced from her husband—who, as I said, used to beat her. Later, however—" Again he raised the listless hand. "Later I discovered that he beat her because she *wanted* to be beaten, but that's another story. It's also beside the point, which is my profession and what I'm doing about it. And what I've done about it since I married Katherine is absolutely nothing. Trying to help her hang onto her sanity was a full-time job, and more. Luckily she had enough money to make it feasible."

"Did you try a psychiatrist?"

"Her psychiatry bill," he answered in a totally uninflected voice, "was about five hundred dollars a month. And the drug bill another hundred."

I sighed, glancing at my watch. It was ten minutes after four. "I repeat what I said, Mr. Cross: If I were you, tomorrow morning I'd shower and shave and put on some clean clothes and go to a barber. Then I'd get back to being an interior decorator, whatever that involves."

With his head still resting against the chair-top, still in profile to me, neck arched and lips slightly pursed, he said quietly, "What's mostly involved, Lieutenant, is bullshit. Most of the clients are either blue-haired old ladies with nothing but coupons to clip, or else they're people like Katherine—rich enough to afford a decorator, and so insecure that it's impossible for them to decide between one piece of furniture and another."

"I'm trying to figure out," I said slowly, "whether you were really very fond of your wife."

For a moment there was silence. Then, very softly, he asked, "Are you married, Lieutenant?" As he said it, he opened his eyes and rolled his head toward me, meeting my gaze directly.

I felt my mouth curving in a wry, knowing smile. I heard myself snort softly, scoring a point for Cross. "It just occurs to me," I said, "that we've gotten off the point, which is June Towers."

"There isn't anything to say. She started out by baby-sitting Steffie while I took Katherine to her psychiatric appointments, which we scheduled at four o'clock to coincide with June's school day. Then, as Katherine got worse, June used to come every afternoon to help with dinner. Sometimes she ate with us, too."

"How long did this arrangement continue?"

"For almost a year, altogether."

"And you paid her twenty dollars a week."

He nodded. He'd closed his eyes again, once more facing the ceiling. He seemed completely relaxed, utterly at ease. He reminded me of a sad, tired man lying limp in a barber's chair.

"Did she work for you after your wife died?"

"Yes. Steffie—liked June. So June came every day for a couple of hours. To fix dinner—and just be here."

"How long has your stepdaughter been gone?"

"Three months."

"June didn't come here after Steffie left?"

"There was no reason to."

"How would you describe June Towers, Mr. Cross? What kind of a girl was she?"

For a moment he didn't reply. Then he said, "She was just—just average. Just a teen-aged girl. She didn't say much. She wasn't lazy, but she wasn't ambitious either. She was a quiet girl."

"Was she especially frugal? Did you get the impression that she saved most of the money you gave her?"

"I wouldn't have any idea, Lieutenant. None."

"Was she pretty, would you say?"

"Pretty enough," he answered indifferently.

39

"Did you ever meet Kent Miller? Her boyfriend?"

"A few times."

"Did you get the impression that they were pretty tight, as the kids say?"

"Pretty involved with each other, you mean?"

"Yes."

He paused before saying heavily, "I guess I'm not really a competent judge, Lieutenant, because I didn't really pay much attention to June Towers—or to anyone or anything except my wife. I was only married to Katherine for two years. But it seems like an eternity, even now. It was totally demanding, living with a neurotic. It's an experience that takes everything out of you."

I rose, picking up my hat. "I've got to be going, Mr. Cross." I laid my card on the coffee table beside a food-caked plate. "If you think of anything that might help us, I'd appreciate a call. Meanwhile, as I said, I'd get back into the swing of things if I were you. Your wife's gone. You've got yourself to think about."

With an effort, sighing deeply, he got to his feet and turned toward the door. I had the feeling that he'd make himself a drink as soon as I left.

Seven

I took a chair on Friedman's right: the "brass's chair." Whenever possible, Friedman called informal meetings in his office, giving himself the pleasure of his oversized swivel chair. The only other armchair was reserved for the visiting officer, usually me. Inspectors were relegated to the straight-backed chairs.

"While all of you have been running aimlessly out in the field," Friedman announced, "I have been laboring behind closed doors, with very promising results, if I do say so."

Canelli, typically, was looking at Friedman with an expectant, hopeful expression. Markham's expression, typically, was inscrutable. Markham was waiting to be shown.

"First," Friedman said, "I located the popcorn vendor and had him brought downtown. It turns out that after twenty years in this country he still can't speak good English. He's Greek. His name is Stavos Papadopolous, and he's saving his money to go back to Greece because he's decided that he doesn't like America. So . . ."

"This is beginning to sound like a Canelli-type prologue," I murmured.

"I'm merely setting the scene," Friedman replied blandly.

"As you'll see. To continue, Mr. Papadopolous, after fifteen minutes of skillful questioning, finally remembered seeing the girl."

"Are you sure?" I asked.

"Definitely. For one thing, he remembered her car—color, make, everything. He remembered the girl, too. No question. He said that she parked near his popcorn wagon a little after four-thirty. He remembers the time because he packed up and left about four forty-five. He says that she parked and just sat in her car—as if she were waiting for someone. When he left the area, she was still parked—presumably still waiting to meet someone. By that time, according to Mr. Papadopolous, it was starting to get dark."

"What about corroborating witnesses?" I asked.

Friedman spread his hands, shaking his head. I turned inquiringly to Markham, who also shook his head.

"Did Mr. Papadopolous see anyone else?" I asked.

"That," Friedman said, "took another half-hour. But I finally got the descriptions of four people who were more or less known to Mr. Papadopolous. That is, they were regulars in the park and he knew them by sight. He never did talk to any of them, and if you'd ever talked to Mr. Papadopolous, you'd understand why. Anyhow, one of these parties we've more or less identified as Lester Farley, who you already know about. Apparently Farley was loitering around between four and four-thirty, then he left. Of course, he could've come back. And he was definitely there during the same time as the victim."

"Anything more from Farley's tail?"

"Culligan called in just a few minutes ago. He didn't get anything but a couple of sore feet. He found a talkative neighbor, though. Apparently Farley is a forty-one-year-old mamma's boy who doesn't like either girls or boys. The last job he held was at Macy's tie counter."

"Does Records have anything on him?"

"As a matter of fact," he answered, "Records *does* have something on him. It seems that when Farley was twelve years old he set a neighbor's cat on fire."

42

"It's like I said," Canelli offered. "He's kinky."

"Why don't we keep him under surveillance until bedtime?" I said to Friedman.

"Suits me."

"Fine. What about the coroner's report?"

"Preliminarily, he hasn't got any surprises for us. She wasn't raped, and probably hadn't had intercourse previous to being murdered. She wasn't a virgin. Death was caused by a massive cerebral hemorrhage resulting from three or four heavy blows to the left side of the head toward the front, indicating that the murderer, if he faced her, is probably right-handed—and probably strong. There weren't any other marks on the body. No fist marks or scratches. Nothing. No needle marks either. However, the right shoulder strap of her bra was broken. Which could, of course, mean anything. I took the time to examine her before they stripped her, though, and it looked to me like someone might've grabbed her clothing in front—holding her, you see, while he hit her. He could've . . ."

The phone rang. It was for me. Friedman signaled for me to take it.

"Lieutenant Hastings? Sorry to interrupt. This is Gerry Olsen, Lieutenant, in the crime lab. I don't know whether you remember me, sir. I'm new here. But—"

"I remember you, Olsen. What is it?"

"Well, I just wanted to tell you, sir, that we're finished with the June Towers car."

"And?"

"Well, we got quite a few prints, at least four different sets."

"Anything to identify who was the last one to drive the car?"

"Well, sir, I don't think it's exactly my place to say."

"Guess, then."

"Well, if I had to guess, I'd say no. Everything on the rim of the steering wheel was pretty well smeared."

"What about the ignition key?"

"We didn't find one, sir."

"Anything else of interest besides the prints?"

"Well, again, sir, I don't think I should . . ."

"All right, Olsen. Have you sent the prints to Classification?"

"Yessir. Forty-five minutes ago."

"Okay. Good. Send the rest of the information to my office."

I hung up.

"Anything?" Friedman asked laconically.

"No. Olsen is a very careful man."

"In this business, that's a virtue."

"Have you got anything else?" I asked Friedman.

"As a matter of fact, I have."

"Good." I settled back in my chair.

"First," Friedman said, "Mr. Papadopolous mentioned three other regulars. There was a man and a boy who spent some time in the area. They come almost every Sunday, Mr. Papadopolous said, and two or three times during the week if the weather's good. The man is in his middle thirties, dark hair, weighing probably a hundred seventy-five. The boy is nine or ten. They were just fooling around, according to Mr. Papadopolous. However, he's sure they were in the area after four forty-five, so they might've seen something. He mentioned that they were 'playing around the trees,' whatever that means."

"How do we find them, though?"

"I've applied myself to that problem," Friedman said, "and I finally prevailed on Mr. Papadopolous to return to the area every day this week, as a public service. He'll be there tomorrow. Someone should be on stakeout with him, obviously." He glanced at Canelli, who in turn glanced appealingly at me. I looked away.

"Also," Friedman was saying, "Mr. Papadopolous remembers seeing the victim talking to a kid on a motorcycle."

I looked up. "Did he describe the kid?"

"A teen-ager, blond, with medium-length hair about to the bottom of the ear. He seemed to know the victim. He rode up to her car, and apparently they talked for a couple of minutes. Then he rode off. He was wearing one of those fringed leather jackets and brown cowboy boots. No helmet."

"What about the motorcycle?" I asked. "Did he describe that?"

"No. He thinks it might've been red. Or maybe orange. Anyhow, it was a bright color, he thinks."

"That motorcycle rider," I said, "sounds like Kent Miller. The victim's boyfriend." I briefly described my interview with the Miller boy. "The time would fit," I said.

Friedman nodded. "It would indeed. Are you saying he could be a suspect?"

I shrugged. "For openers, he specifically stated that he didn't see June yesterday."

"Hmm."

"What else have you got?"

"Nothing, really. Except that I talked to Randall Grant for a while—the victim's stepfather. He came down to make the identification."

"What'd you think of him?" I asked.

"I thought he was a horse's ass," Friedman replied promptly.

"What's he do for a living?"

"Sells real estate, supposedly. But he reminds me of one of those bartenders who spends all his time down at the end of the bar, scowling at the customers."

"Did he give you any new ideas about the victim—why anyone would want to murder her?"

"No," Friedman answered. "But I was interested in what he had to say—especially *how* he said it and *when* he said it, which was just a couple of minutes after he'd identified the body."

"What'd you mean?"

"I mean that he seemed to be talking about a neighbor kid—someone he just knew slightly."

"That's the way he acted when I broke the news to him—like the whole thing was a plot to annoy him."

"I wish," Friedman said thoughtfully, "that we could get a better personality profile on June Towers. I mean, all I get is a picture of some faceless teen-aged chick with three hundred bucks taped under her bed. Nobody loves her, nobody hates her. Nobody knows much about her. Not really."

"There," I said, "I agree with you. We've got to know more about her." I turned to Canelli. "What'd you find out?"

"Well—" Frowning earnestly, Canelli hunched forward in his chair. "Most of the neighbors said she was just an ordinary girl, like you said. She wasn't noisy and she didn't give anyone any trouble. There's one old lady, though, who lives three doors down from the Grants on the opposite side. She said that June Towers was 'foxy,' as she put it. She's about eighty. The informant, I mean. And she's one of these real sharp little old ladies. You know—kind of skinny and quick-moving, with an eye like a bird, or something."

"What does she mean by 'foxy'?" Friedman asked. In his voice I could plainly hear the elaborately patient, ironic note that he reserved especially for questioning Canelli.

"Well, you know—" Canelli shrugged. "Just foxy. Tricky, I guess you'd say."

"Did she mention anything specific?"

"No, it was just a feeling she had. I gather that she spends a lot of her time looking out the window."

"If we didn't have window watchers and paid stoolies," Friedman observed, "we'd have to triple the force. Overnight."

"Anything else?" I asked Canelli.

"Well, I spotted a couple of teen-aged girls hanging around the victim's house. They'd just heard the news, and they came by for a look, I guess. I talked to them one at a time. One of them—her name was Cindy—she was one of those weepy types who won't say anything bad about the dead. And all the time she's sniffling you know she's really enjoying herself. But the other one—she was a cute little Chinese girl named Lillian—she was a lot sharper and a lot cooler. She said that June Towers was one of those kids who's always thinking. She didn't talk much, and she didn't laugh much either. She kept to herself. But according to Lillian, she was pretty good at getting what she wanted. Like boys, for instance. Lillian didn't say so in so many words, but I got the feeling that when June decided she wanted a guy, she just put out for him. And that was that. No fuss."

"How about the money?"

"I asked Lillian about that. All she said was that if June had

46

figured out some angle, she sure wouldn't go around advertising."

"That," Friedman said, "is the first bit of information that . . ."

The phone rang. Again it was for me. It was Manley in Communications, saying, "I know you're in conference, Lieutenant. But I've got a breather on the phone. He—or she—wants to talk to whoever's in charge of the Towers investigation. I thought I should at least tell you."

"I'll take it. Be sure and record the call."

"Yessir."

A moment later a disguised voice whispered in my ear, "If you want to find the girl's murderer, go to 727 Twenty-fifth Avenue." The line clicked dead.

I replaced the receiver and repeated the message to the others.

"They're beginning to come out of the woodwork," Friedman commented, "right on schedule. It's the power of TV."

I said, "Still, I might as well check it out." And to Canelli: "We can find out what it's all about, then call it a day—or a night." I was thinking of Ann, and our movie. I turned to Markham. "Did you find out anything in the park?"

Sitting a little straighter in his chair, unconsciously lifting his chin against the tug of his gleaming white collar, Markham said, "Not really. I had six men, and we covered everything in a two-hundred-foot radius of the body, looking for the weapon. No luck."

"Was the terrain a problem?"

He nodded decisively. "Definitely. Parts of that park are like a jungle."

For a moment we all shared a long, thoughtful silence. Finally Friedman said, "If we knew where she got that money, we'd be a lot further along."

"I'd also like to know," Markham said, "whether the murderer took her car."

"It's a reasonable assumption," I answered. "Her folding

47

money and her car key were missing. All she had in her purse was a latchkey."

"You're saying that's the motive then: the money and her car." His voice was flat, his sidelong glance plainly doubtful. Playing the percentages, Markham was a squad-room skeptic. He constantly sought to identify a certain theory with a certain colleague, on the simple premise that most theories were eventually wrong. Meanwhile, Markham tried to avoid committing himself until the last possible moment. It was a delicate, difficult game, but he was good at it.

"No," I answered quietly, "I'm just saying that whoever took her key probably took her car. What I'd *really* like to know is why the car was abandoned so close to the scene."

Listening, Friedman had been poking a hole in a fresh cigar, using a straightened paper clip. "What I'd like to know," he said, "is why the Miller kid said he didn't see her yesterday, when maybe he did."

I got to my feet. "I'm beginning to wonder about that phone tip, since 727 Twenty-fifth Avenue is in the victim's neighborhood. I'm also beginning to get hungry."

"What about another meeting tomorrow morning?" Friedman said. "Maybe someone'll have a brainstorm in the meantime."

Nodding agreement, I turned toward the door.

Eight

As I pressed the doorbell at 727 Twenty-fifth Avenue, I automatically checked my watch. The time was 6:00 P.M.; the sky was already dark. The house was lit in almost every room.

As a precaution, I gestured Canelli to stand off to my right, ready. With jackets unbuttoned, we loosened our service revolvers. Almost immediately the porch light came on and the door latch clicked.

A bulky, balding man of about forty opened the door. With his heavy shoulders hunched aggressively forward, head lowered on a short, muscular neck, he looked like an overweight, out-of-shape linebacker—slow to start but hard to stop.

I showed him the shield, identified myself, and asked for his name. I watched his gray eyes look us over, taking his time. His face was muscle-bunched, like his shoulders. His sparse hair was faded-red, his eyebrows ginger. His complexion was ruddy and freckle-flecked, seamed by the sun and wind. He was a stolid, stubborn-looking man.

"My name is Fisher," he said finally. "Bill Fisher. What's it all about, anyhow?" He asked the question truculently, meeting my eye with a faintly annoyed frown. "We're just about to sit down to dinner."

"This won't take more than a few minutes, Mr. Fisher. If we could come inside, I'll explain."

Momentarily he hesitated, then stood aside. I walked into a living room crowded with Early American furniture and dominated by a huge color TV, also Early American. Everything was elaborately ruffled: lampshades, furniture trim, curtains. An expensive book on American antiques was prominently displayed on the coffee table, but a second look confirmed that the furniture was factory-made.

As I stood looking around the room, a woman wearing a ruffled apron entered from the dining room, standing in the connecting archway. She looked questioningly at her husband. She was a trim, attractive brunette with shrewd eyes and a tight mouth. She had the unmistakable air of a housewife interrupted at the wrong time.

"These men are from the police," the husband said shortly. "This is my wife, Marge."

Smiling at her, I remained standing while she perched on a straight-backed chair. Her husband stood beside her, pointedly not asking us to sit down. Sighing, I seated myself on the sofa. Canelli stood propped in the archway leading into the hall. He'd forgotten to button his jacket, and I could plainly see the butt of his gun. Frowning, I stared at his waist. Following my gaze, he came to haphazard attention, buttoning his jacket.

As I turned to face Bill Fisher I said, "I'm sure you know that a neighbor of yours was a homicide victim. June Towers."

I watched the woman catch her breath sharply, then glance at her husband, still standing impassively at her side. With obvious effort, rigidly controlling himself, he continued to look directly into my eyes, projecting a slowly gathering sense of outraged puzzlement.

It was a good, gutsy performance. But his acting partner had already blown the scene.

"Have you caught whoever did it?" Fisher asked, his voice still steady.

50

"No, we haven't. That's why we're here, Mr. Fisher. We're in the process of sorting everything out—checking all the leads as they come in to us."

I saw Marge Fisher's lips move soundlessly before she finally managed to say, "B—but wh-what do you want? I mean, you certainly don't—" She couldn't finish it. Now her wide, incredulous eyes were rapidly circling the room. I'd seen the same desperate expression in the eyes of accident victims about to lose consciousness—trying to see it all, racing that final moment of oblivion.

"An anonymous telephone caller said that someone at this address could give us information concerning the death of June Towers." I looked silently from the husband to the wife. It was time for me to wait—and watch.

The man looked as if he were gathering himself to bluff it out, blustering about his rights, and the taxes he pays, and the friends he had at City Hall.

The woman, though, was transparently frightened. She was losing control of her writhing fingers and her tight, twitching lips. I noticed that her glance strayed repeatedly toward the hallway stairs leading up to the second story.

"Is there anyone else in the house, Mr. Fisher?" I asked.

The question seemed suddenly to deflate him. He looked aside at his wife, then sighed heavily.

It was the wife who answered. In a low voice she said, "My son and my brother-in-law are upstairs."

Having said it, she slumped back in the chair. Her shoulders went slack, her head hung listlessly forward, eyes averted. Now her fingers lay inert in her lap. Her battle was over.

Beside her, the husband was shifting his feet as his gaze, too, was involuntarily drawn up toward the ceiling.

Addressing the man, I asked, "Do you mind if I go upstairs and talk to your son and your brother?"

As he crossed to a ruffled love seat and sank down, he shook his head sharply. "Go ahead," he said shortly, suddenly scowling at me. "I don't give a damn; go ahead."

"Thank you." As I passed Canelli, I moved my head to the

Fishers, indicating that he should begin questioning them. Then I climbed the thickly carpeted hallway stairs.

It was a three-bedroom house, with a spacious upstairs bath done entirely in pink and cream tile. The first bedroom door on my right was perhaps eight inches ajar. From inside, I could hear voices.

I knocked softly.

Immediately the voices were silent. All sound of movement ceased.

Unbuttoning my coat, I knocked again. On the other side of the door I could hear someone clearing his throat. Slowly I pushed the door open.

The bedroom was furnished for a boy. Posters and pennants were arranged on the walls; models and toys were displayed on shelves and tables. Yet something essential was missing. Looking around a second time, I decided that the room was too orderly. Either the boy was abnormally neat, or his mother constantly picked up after him. Or both.

The room was dimly lit. On the far side a boy and a man were seated on either side of a small worktable, beneath a lonely cone of bright white light. The boy had Bill Fisher's carrot hair and freckled face, but his eyes were darker, more sensitive. His mouth was softer, his arms slimmer, his neck skinnier in proportion to his head.

Except for his dark hair, the man bore a marked resemblance to the boy. Both were slim, delicately built. Both were staring at me with almost identical expressions of anxious, timid concern.

Advancing into the room, I quietly closed the door behind me and turned first to the man. I introduced myself and stated my business. I realized that I was speaking very softly, as if I'd just entered a sickroom. As I repeated the routine phrases, I was thinking of Mr. Papadopolous' "regulars"—the man and the boy who often came to the park together.

When I'd finished talking, the man simply sat as he had before, staring at me with dark, sad eyes. Nothing I'd said had caused even the slightest flicker of interest or surprise, least of all the mention of June Towers' death.

"May I have your name, sir?" I asked.

His voice was almost a whisper as he answered, "It's Fisher. James Fisher."

"Age?"

"Thirty-eight."

"Occupation?"

A moment of silent, regretful resignation. Then: "I'm unemployed."

"What's your profession, Mr. Fisher? Your line of work?"

He studied me for a long moment before saying quietly, "I don't have a profession, Lieutenant. Or a line of work, either." Another moment of contemplation followed, during which he looked at me with the detached, dispassionate expression of a monk sworn to silence. His eyes never left mine. His body hadn't shifted; his hands hadn't stirred. Finally he said, "Until three months ago I was an inmate at the State Rehabilitation Facility at Graceville." He waited politely while the institution's significance registered on me. Then he said, "I was committed to the facility twenty-six months ago, when I was judged criminally insane. It was a San Mateo County case."

I turned immediately to the boy. "What's your name, son?"

"D—" He swallowed. "David. It's David. David Fisher."

"How old are you, David?"

"I—I'm almost ten."

I smiled at him. "I wonder whether you'd mind if I talked with your uncle for a few minutes, David? In private."

He started to say something, then shrugged uncertainly. Finally he nodded his head. His eyes had grown very large. His mouth hung slightly open.

"Good." I stepped close beside him, gesturing for him to rise. As he got obediently to his feet, I said, "You go downstairs, David. Your parents are down there with Inspector Canelli. He's a detective. I'll be down in a few minutes."

He stood perfectly still for a moment, staring wordlessly up at me with an utterly blank expression. Then he turned his whole body to face his uncle.

The man smiled wearily. "It's all right, David. I'll tell you everything that happens. I promise."

"But . . ."

"It's all right. You don't have to worry."

The boy walked slowly to the door. In the doorway he turned, staring at his uncle. I saw James Fisher smile slightly, then slowly nod. The boy closed the door. I waited for the soft sound of his footsteps on the thick stairway carpet before I sat down to face the uncle across the linoleum-topped worktable. The table was strewn with miscellaneous radio parts and a plan for an elementary receiver. My own son, years ago, had tried to build a similar receiver. He'd never finished it. I'd offered to help him, but he hadn't accepted the offer. Later—much later—I realized that he'd probably known the offer was perfunctory—a well-meant fraud.

I raised my eyes to meet those of James Fisher. His gaze was unwavering. According to the squad-room cliché, a detective has only two essential tools of the trade: his gun and his long, cold stare. Of the two, the latter is more important.

Yet when James Fisher's eyes finally fell, he seemed merely bored with the game—indifferent, totally unintimidated.

I decided to give him his constitutional rights. Still the dark, impassive eyes revealed nothing. In reply, he said, "Miranda and Escobosa have helped the common man more than Sacco and Vanzetti. Did you ever think about that, Lieutenant?"

"As a matter of fact," I answered, "I never did."

"Yet Sacco was better than Miranda, and Vanzetti was a better man than Escobosa. It's the times, though—the times were worse, so the men had to be better. Now the times are better. But only easier, not really better. So, actually, they're worse. Which means that . . ."

I drew a deep breath. "Would you mind telling me, Mr. Fisher, the nature of the charge against you? The San Mateo charge, I mean—the one on which you were sentenced."

54

"It was aggravated assault." His voice was totally uninflected.

"What was the nature of the crime?"

The pale, haunted face stirred into a wan imitation of exhausted amusement. "Do you want my version, Lieutenant? Or the prosecution's?"

"Yours."

He nodded gravely, now mocking me faintly as he said, "Twenty-six months ago it would have taken me an hour to tell you about it. Now I can do it in a minute—one short, concise minute."

I answered his nod. "Fine."

"At the time," he said slowly, "I was a paranoid schizophrenic—according to my lawyer's psychiatrist, anyhow. We were living in Redwood City. All of us—just like we're living now. David was only six then, and he couldn't understand what was happening to me. And I couldn't tell him, because it would've frightened him. So I stayed in my room and wrestled in the night with my demons. Slowly, of course, the demons began to win—as demons always will when they're only in your mind. Finally they began driving me from my room, which was my last hope—my last line of defense. At first I thought it was only a strategic retreat—that I'd eventually outwit them by running. Then I realized that although they didn't follow me outside, they were waiting for me when I returned to my room. I was playing their game—which, of course, always happens. Still, it was wonderful to find some peace during the night, even if it was alone, outside—even if I knew they'd be waiting for me at home. But then, of course, the inevitable happened." He drew a deep regretful breath.

I decided to say nothing, waiting for what I knew must surely follow.

"My demons finally followed me outside—out into the night. And then, of course, it was hopeless." His voice began to drop. "There was no place to run—or, at least, I didn't think there was. I—I can remember that terrible feeling of waiting. I decided to wait for them in the park. I can remember feeling that when it happened, I wanted it to happen in the park. Because even then I used to take David to the park. So during the day, you see, it was a different place—sunny and bright and laughing. It—" Suddenly he stopped speaking. He was staring down at his hands, clasped like a penitent's on the table before him.

"What were you waiting for?" My voice, I realized, was as quiet as my victim's.

"I was waiting for them to touch me," he said simply. "Every night I could feel them coming closer. Until one night they touched me. But—" He sighed deeply. "But of course, they weren't really my demons after all. They were just three teenagers—two boys and a girl—out for a night's fun."

"And you attacked one of them."

He raised his dead-calm eyes, empty of hope. He simply nodded.

"Which one did you attack?"

"It—it was very dark, Lieutenant. But it was the girl."

I nodded. It was all together now—the park, the female victim, even, indirectly, the boy. And the darkness. Not the night, but the darkness.

"Are you aware," I began, "that June Towers was murdered yesterday evening in Golden Gate Park?"

"I heard about it," he answered calmly. "But I don't know what happened."

"I'll tell you what happened later, Mr. Fisher. But first I'd like you to account for your movements yesterday, from, say, four o'clock until six o'clock."

"I can do that very easily, Lieutenant. I was with David."

"During those hours?"

"We left the house in the afternoon after lunch. We—" He hesitated. "We played together in the park until it got dark. Then we came home."

"At about what time did you get home?"

He shrugged. "I'm afraid time isn't the same for me as it is for you, Lieutenant. We don't use the same measure."

"Was it after five o'clock?" I pressed.

"I'm sorry, I can't say."

56

"Was it dark—fully dark—when you got home?"

Helplessly he shook his head. Now his eyes were looking far away, unfocused. He seemed to be losing interest in my questions, as a child might lose interest in a dull game.

"Was anyone at home, here, when the two of you arrived?"

He nodded vaguely. "My sister-in-law was at home. She can tell you what you want to know. Time is very important to my sister-in-law."

"I'd like you to tell me exactly what you and David did yesterday—from the time you left here until the time you returned." I spread my notebook on the worktable, pen poised.

"Well, first we went to feed the ducks," he answered dreamily. "We used the last of David's allowance to buy some stale bread, and we fed the ducks. Then we watched the model sailboat races for a while. And then we walked over to the polo field and watched them fly model airplanes. And—" He paused, frowning. "And that's all we did."

"Do you remember passing by a popcorn-vendor's wagon on your way home?"

He brightened. "Yes, I do. That's when we stopped to watch the squirrel. It was just beginning to get dark. And that's the best time to watch squirrels."

"You watched this squirrel in the area near the popcorn wagon?"

"Yes."

"Did you feed the squirrel? Or just watch it?"

"We just watched it."

"Were you together the whole time?"

Frowning, he looked up. "I—I'm afraid I don't understand."

Conscious of a sudden, irrational goad of uncontrollable irritation, I said sharply, "It's a simple enough question. I'm asking you whether, when you were watching this squirrel, you and David were together the whole time."

Suddenly downcast, he sat slowly shaking his head, mumbling that he didn't remember. He was avoiding my eyes, plainly hurt. My moment's surrender to pique had snapped something essential between us: that delicate, tenuous filament that binds inquisitor and victim together in some strange, necessary union.

It was time to go.

As I rose to my feet I was aware that now I felt a sense of sadness, just as irrational as the previous moment's sudden anger.

I folded my notebook together, clicked my ballpoint pen, and returned both to my jacket pocket. Pitching my voice to an impersonal note, I said, "We'll be checking on your story, Mr. Fisher. It will probably take us a day or two. We'll probably want you to come downtown to be interviewed and identified. Do you understand?"

"Yes. You're talking about a line-up. And long hours of questioning in small rooms."

"It's the only way we can get the job done, Mr. Fisher. A girl has been murdered. I have to find out why—and how."

"Yes, I can see that." He nodded.

"Good." As I left the room, he was sitting exactly as I'd first seen him a half-hour ago—a lonely figure beneath a cone of cold white light. He was staring expressionlessly at the boy's empty chair.

Nine

As I got into the cruiser beside Canelli, the time was ten minutes after seven. Allowing fifteen minutes for business, I could go home, wash my face and change my shirt, and pick up Ann by eight o'clock.

"Well," I asked Canelli, "what'd you find out?"

"From the kid, you mean?"

"Yes."

While I fidgeted, Canelli took five full minutes to outline, with embellishments, David Fisher's movements during the critical three hours of the previous day. The boy's account tallied with his uncle's in almost every particular.

When Canelli finally finished, I sat for a moment in thoughtful silence, deciding whether to call in for a stakeout. I thought of the Lester Farley stakeout, still with several hours to run. A homicide detail, like every other department of municipal government, must ultimately answer to the efficiency expert, whose sole concern is how many man-hours are required to solve a given crime. The fewer the man-hours, the better the officer's record looks when promotions come around.

"What about the time that they were watching the squirrel?" I asked. "That's the critical point."

Canelli nodded. "Yeah. Right. And that kid, you know, is pretty smart. He's real fond of his uncle, that's for sure. And the kid knew all about the murder, and where it was committed, and all. And it didn't take him two seconds, probably, to figure out that we suspected the uncle. So right away he says that he had his uncle eyeballed right from the second they left the house until the second they got back."

"Do you think he was lying?"

"I don't know," Canelli answered slowly. "I couldn't decide. With kids, it's hard to tell, at least for me. And he's one of these quiet, saucer-eyed kids with lots of imagination. You can tell that about half the time he's living in some kind of a dream world all his own, and making up stories that he tells to himself and everyone else, if they ask him."

"Did you get a chance to talk to the parents separately?"

"No. I didn't have the time. And besides, I know that it's tricky where kids are concerned. I remembered that hassle you had a couple of months ago, and . . ." He stopped speaking—having already said too much.

"I think," I said, "that we'd better set up an interrogation for the whole Fisher family—all four of them. At the office, about eleven tomorrow morning. We'll plan on having a staff meeting in my office about ten." I glanced moodily at the Fisher house, again conscious of the dull, unfocused anger I'd felt interviewing James Fisher. Friedman had once remarked that there was no sport in putting the arm on a looney. Friedman's flip, throwaway remarks often had the cold, hard ring of truth.

I glanced again at my watch. "I'd like to have you drop me at my place and then come back here and tell the Fishers about the interrogation tomorrow. That is, if you don't mind. I, ah, have something to do."

"Sure," he answered cheerfully, switching on the engine. "No sweat." He got the car under way with a series of lurches, then asked, "Do you think Fisher is our man, Lieutenant?"

60

"I don't know," I answered shortly. "Suddenly this case is going too many directions at once."

"Well," Canelli said, "that's better than no place at once."

I glanced at him, sighed, and settled back in the seat. I suddenly felt tired. At age forty-three, after a hard day, I should be returning home for a late dinner, an hour of newspapers and TV, and a good night's sleep. Instead, like someone half my age, I would only be home long enough to change my shirt. And at that, I could be late picking up Ann.

Ten

I closed the passenger's door, rounded the car and slipped behind the wheel. The time was just after midnight.

"If you don't have to be home," I said, "let's go to my place. I've got some Hennessey four-star."

I saw her smile. "What you're really saying," she said, "is 'my place or yours.' "

"I guess I am, at that." As I started the engine, I studied her shadowed profile. I'd known her for more than a month. I'd seen her three or four times a week. Yet her wide forehead, her small, straight nose, and her firm chin still seemed subtly different each time I really looked at her.

It had been in the line of duty that I'd met her. My first cop's impression, neatly categorized, had been of a small, stylish blonde named Ann Haywood—a grammar-school teacher, the divorced wife of a society psychiatrist, the mother of two overprivileged sons, ages ten and sixteen. She'd been in trouble when I'd met her, and she could hardly smile. But as the danger to her family passed, she'd slowly revealed a quiet, subtle sense of low-keyed humor. She was a very private person. She seldom laughed, but she often smiled.

"Your place, then," she said. "But I have to be home some-time. Dan's out with his father, for a late night, but he'll be home. He might be home now, in fact."

"Where's Billy?"

"Spending the night with a friend. They're studying their lines for the fifth-grade play."

"Good."

We were driving slowly down Union Street. Even on a Monday night it was thronged with bar-hopping pleasure-seekers, most of them dressed in the latest with-it fashion. Bar for bar, smile for smile, more pickups were consummated on sophisticated Union Street than in the Tenderloin.

"You're quiet tonight," she said. "Quieter than usual, that is."

Rather than reply, I simply looked at her, smiling. Sharing a silence was something we did well together.

"I thought policemen didn't personalize their work," she said finally. Her voice was bantering, friendly.

"We don't."

"You are, though. You're wrapped in a dark, mysterious cloak."

I sighed.

"The reason I'm bugging you about it," she persisted, "is that I teach in the district where June Towers was murdered. Did you know that?"

"Well, I . . ."

"I'm the victim of natural human curiosity. Plus my students are the victims of a sordid, morbid preoccupation with vi-olence, entirely natural to children. If they knew—if they should ever find out—that I was actually driving down Union Street with the stern godlike creature who . . ."

"Did you ever have a boy named David Fisher for a student?" I interrupted. My voice, I knew, was harsher than I'd intended. I never like to discuss business after hours.

"I taught him last year." She paused. Then, in a lower, graver voice, she said, "Is David involved?"

I hesitated, sorting out my personal motives and professional obligations as we drove a long stop-and-go-block in silence. I could feel her eyes on me, waiting patiently.

"David's uncle could be involved," I answered shortly.

To my surprise, she didn't reply. I saw that she was biting her lips, looking straight ahead.

"What is it?" I asked.

She drew a deep breath. "Teachers personalize, even if detective lieutenants don't. And it just so happens that David's always had a—a kind of stray-puppydog appeal for me, probably because he doesn't seem to have much of an appeal for anyone else."

"Oh?"

We'd arrived at our turnoff; three more blocks and I'd be home. Ahead, two young girls in a seven-thousand-dollar Porsche were waving wildly to friends on the sidewalk.

"What about the uncle, James Fisher?" I asked. "Did David ever mention him?"

"Yes, he did." Apprehension was plain in her voice.

"What'd he say about him?"

She drew a deep breath, then said, "About a month ago I happened to see David after school. He's very good at drawing and stays after school for the art club twice a week. He told me that his uncle had just come to live with them. He was elated about it—quietly elated. I had the feeling that"—she paused briefly—"that his uncle means a great deal to him."

I turned into the last block, searching for a parking place. "What kind of a kid is David?" I asked casually. "Is he honest, would you say?"

"Yes," she answered readily, "I *would* say. I'd also say that he's intelligent, sensitive, and very easily hurt—probably because he's been hurt so often. He's one of those kids that other children love to torment, simply because he doesn't defend himself."

"Thus his stray-puppydog appeal." As I said it, I was sorry, realizing I was far from expressing the balanced detachment I'd hoped to project.

In the next block I saw a parking space. I laboriously

64

wedged my car into the spot, bumper-thumping too loudly, front and back. Only after I'd switched off the engine did I realize that she hadn't spoken.

She was looking out into the night, as if we were still driving and she were watching the road. Her voice was very low as she said, "Until right now I never realized how—how difficult it must be to be a policeman. You've always got to be on guard against your—your finer feelings."

"You're right," I said. "That's all I can say—you're right. But if you're really saying that cops don't *have* finer feelings, then you're wrong."

I felt her turn toward me. "Frank, I didn't mean . . ."

"Eight hours a day—and sometimes a lot longer—I spend my time with either the victims of violent crime or the criminals responsible. If I wasted my energy on either sympathy or rage, I'd never get the job done." I said it in a flat, impersonal voice—my interrogation-room voice. I'd meant for it to sound different.

"God," she said softly, "it must be hard."

"It *is* hard. But there's a satisfaction in it—just like there is in any job, if you're good at it."

I felt her hand on my arm. It was a light, delicate touch, hardly a caress. Yet somehow, at that moment, it was more than a caress.

"Come on," she whispered, "let's go in. You promised me some Hennessey."

"What time is it?" she whispered.

I glanced across her at the bedside clock. "Two-thirty. I wish you could stay."

"But I can't. Would you like to come to dinner Thursday night?"

"If I can manage it, yes."

"Considering that I first met you while you were menacing my firstborn, the boys are very fond of you—in a gruff, manly way. Not to mention me."

"But not gruffly."

"No, not gruffly."

"Good."

A moment of silence. Then: "I'm sorry for what I said about your finer feelings, Frank. It—it didn't turn out the way I meant it. I was trying to—to pay you a compliment."

"I know. Don't worry about it. Please."

"You *are* a very warm person. Really. The first time I met you—the very first time—I had the feeling that you cared about what happened to Dan, even though at the time I know it looked as if he—" She didn't finish it.

Moving closer to her, drawing my hand in a slow caress down the curve of her back, finding the full, exciting swell of her flank, I whispered into the hollow of her throat, making a mock-serious declaration: "It was you that I cared about, if you want the truth. From the first moment I saw you standing on your porch and frowning at me, I realized that we were meant for each other."

In response, she sighed softly. I could picture the wistful shadow of a very private regret in her eyes; I could feel the silky muscles of her back shift almost imperceptibly. She was drawing herself together, unconsciously moving away.

"What a shame," she whispered, "that we have to say it flippantly when we talk about each other. We . . ."

I touched her small nose firmly with my forefinger, silencing her. "No introspection. Not in bed. Pillow talk, okay. Even giggling is okay. But not introspection."

I could feel her relaxing; I knew that she was smiling mischievously. Extricating her arm, she pressed my nose painfully with her forefinger. "I've got to go home," she whispered. "Dan will be calling the cops."

Eleven

"I thought you'd scheduled a meeting for ten," Friedman said, exhaling gratefully as he sank heavily into my visitor's chair.

"It's only ten minutes to ten."

"Really?" He frowned down at his watch. "Ever since that last hot pursuit, when I actually had to grapple with the suspect, this thing hasn't been worth a damn. And it's a good watch, too."

"How often do you have it cleaned?"

"Hmm?"

"You should have them cleaned and oiled every two years. There isn't a lubricant made that lasts more than two years."

"About fifteen years ago," he announced, "I had a watch cleaned. I paid twenty-one dollars for the watch and thirteen fifty to have it cleaned. That's the last time I ever had a watch cleaned. It's simple economics."

"Then you'd better start shopping for a new watch."

Grunting as he settled himself in the chair like a burrowing bear, he said, "Anything new?"

I outlined the Fisher interrogation, without mentioning Ann's involvement.

"It sounds," Friedman observed, "like this Fisher's a live one. Did you find out who phoned in the tip?"

"No. But I didn't try. Is there anything on Lester Farley?"

"I just read Culligan's report. It seems that around eleven P.M. Farley left his place and started off for about a seven-mile stroll, some of it through the park. Culligan, I expect, will apply for disability."

"Did Farley do anything but walk?"

"No, nothing. Still, a forty-one-year-old mamma's boy who used to torch cats bears watching."

"Anybody else turn up anything? Any more leads?"

"Yes. Mr. Papadopolous was waiting for me when I arrived this morning. Mr. Papadopolous, in spite of his broken speech and his distaste for American ways, is beginning to get interested in the Towers case. Or maybe he just likes me. Anyhow, after about twenty minutes of conversation it developed that in the wee small hours Mr. Papadopolous was smitten by something he forgot to tell me yesterday. He . . ."

A knock sounded. Canelli and Markham entered, both with manila folders under their arms. When they'd settled themselves, Friedman and I took five minutes to fill them in on the information we'd already exchanged. Friedman described Mr. Papadopolous' visit, finishing with the statement that Mr. Papadopolous had remembered a "dark, suspicious-looking man of middle age sitting near the murder scene in a white car." After some time spent with the car file, Mr. Papadopolous had identified the car as "probably a new Ford." However, Friedman was skeptical of Mr. Papadopolous' expertise concerning American automobiles.

"What about the Fishers?" I asked Canelli.

"They're coming down here in about an hour, Lieutenant. No sweat."

"The boy, too?"

"Yessir."

"How'd they take it when you told them to come down?"

"Well, the woman seemed real upset—wild-eyed in kind of

a quiet way, twisting her hands and swallowing a lot, and every-thing. She looked like she was either going to bust out crying or else cuss me out. And the husband, he was glaring around like he was a—an enraged bull, or something, that couldn't make up his mind what target to go after. So he just kind of glared at me."

Listening, Friedman had been slowly shaking his head. "You do have a lyric gift, Canelli. No question about it."

"What about the boy?" I interposed. "David. Did you talk to him?"

"No, sir. He was upstairs. Talking with the uncle, I guess."

Nodding, I absently riffled through the pages of my notebook, as if I were searching for notes on a new topic. But actually my mind had slipped back to the strange, silent tableau of the boy and the uncle as I'd first seen them seated at the linoleum-topped table, staring at me, their expressions so curiously identical.

Friedman's voice broke into my thoughts. "What about that Miller kid, Frank? Kent Miller. Shouldn't we get him down here and find out whether he met the girl in the park? If he *did* meet her just before the murder, and if he originally denied it, we've got our first real contradiction of testimony."

Looking up from the notebook, I nodded. It was a point I should have made. I turned to Markham.

"Why don't you pick up Kent Miller at Alta High and bring him down here, Jerry? Check with his parents first. If they aren't available, con him into coming—don't force him. And while you're at Alta, see what you can get from the girl's counselor and friends. Ask about money. I keep thinking that she could've been dealing."

Markham rubbed his chin, watching me with cold, remote eyes. I knew that expression. He was thinking that so far I'd as-signed him only the dull, routine tasks that didn't require the tal-ents of an acting sergeant.

He was right. To myself, I could admit it.

I turned to Canelli. "While you're waiting for the Fishers,

why don't you call up the girl's stepfather, Randall Grant, and ask him if he can come downtown? Ask him what kind of a car he has, since he fits Mr. Papadopolous' description. Then do the same for Walter Cross. He's dark and middle-aged—and pretty weird. I'd like to see what he turns into when he's exposed to the sunlight. And I'd like to see how Grant acts, away from his wife. In some ways, his reaction is the strangest of all."

The two inspectors nodded, gathered up their folders, and left the office. Friedman sighed, settled back and lit a cigar. "Well," he said amiably, "this case seems to be going in at least three different directions—at approximately equal rates of speed."

"I said the same thing myself last night."

"We've got James Fisher," Friedman said, raising a pudgy forefinger, "who looks to be about as hot as a prospect can get, except for the alibi of a ten-year-old playmate. We've got Lester Farley"—he raised another finger—"who's a good suspect-type and doesn't even have a kid for an alibi. Then we've got Kent Miller, who's my personal nominee." A third finger joined the other two.

"Why do you say that?"

"When you've been in this business as long as I have, Lieutenant, you'll discover that the suspect who gets caught lying is the suspect who'll eventually earn you a promotion—providing he can't think faster than you can."

"How about a cup of coffee?" I asked.

"Then there's Randall Grant and even Walter Cross," he continued, ignoring my invitation, pausing only to puff on the cigar, "promoted to prominence by Mr. Papadopolous. It's my personal opinion that if it isn't James Fisher, and if for some reason it's not Kent Miller, then it'll probably turn out to be Randall Grant. It'll probably turn out that—"

"Listen, why don't we talk about it over a cup of—"

"—that Grant was screwing the victim while her mother was out at a double feature, or somewhere. That kind of thing happens all the—"

70

Hiding Place

"I'm going. I'll be back in ten minutes."

"Bring me a cup, will you? And a glazed doughnut. Naturally, I'll pay for the doughnut."

"Naturally."

Twelve

I'd already grouped four chairs around my desk when Canelli knocked.

"Come in." As I said it, I rounded my desk and stood behind it, smiling.

Marge Fisher entered first, then the boy, finally the father. Canelli came in last, closed the door and took a seat to my far left. I gestured Mrs. Fisher to a place next to Canelli. Mr. Fisher sat on my far right, with the boy seated between himself and his wife, directly in front of me.

I smiled at the boy. "Hello, David. How are you today?"

"F—" He swallowed. "Fine, sir."

My buzzer sounded. Frowning, I picked up the phone. "Yes?"

"It's Pete, Frank. The uncle is in an interrogation room waiting for me. And now I just heard that Randall Grant is on his way upstairs. So why don't you have Canelli interrogate Grant while I'm questioning James Fisher? Markham's still out at Alta High. You can check with both Canelli and me after you've finished with the Fishers, and before either Grant or James Fisher leave the building. Okay?"

"Yes. Fine. I'll send him in." I hung up and quickly instructed Canelli to check with Lieutenant Friedman. When the door had closed, I turned again to the boy. "I'm sorry, David. I was just going to say that I'd like to have you relax. There's nothing for you to worry about—nothing at all. That's why I've asked your parents to be present. Do you understand?"

"Y—yes."

I pushed the microphone across the desk, pressing the green button. "If you have no objections"—I included them all in the arc of my inquiring glance—"I'd like to record what we say. It saves time."

The parents murmured agreement while the boy mutely stared at the small chrome mike.

"What I'm mostly concerned about, David," I began, "is the time you spent with your uncle on Sunday evening. Between the time you left home and the time you returned. Now, I realize that Inspector Canelli has already asked you all this, just yesterday. But I have to ask you again. Do you understand?"

"I—I guesso."

"All right. Good. Now, first—" I opened my notebook. "First I want to read you what I understand to be a true and complete account of everything you and your uncle did from approximately three P.M. on Sunday, January fourteenth, until approximately six P.M. of that same day. I want you to listen very carefully. Because when I've finished, I'm going to question you about a few points. Do you understand?"

The boy nodded slowly, looking at me with his dark, solemn eyes. Watching him, I unaccountably remembered the postwar CARE ads: the frail, unsmiling child dressed in shabby European clothing and staring with large, tragic eyes from the glossy pages of the best American magazines.

In meticulous detail I reconstructed James Fisher's account of the afternoon in question. As I talked, I looked from the son to the mother to the father. The boy had a fixed expression of apprehensive uncertainty. The mother's anxious eyes darted constantly from her son's face to mine. The father gazed at me with a silent, implacable pugnacity, blinking constantly, continually flexing his thick fingers into chunky fists.

When I'd finished, I allowed a long moment of silence to elapse while I covertly assessed the boy's response to what I'd said. His reaction was predictable: the mute, unrevealing watchfulness of a child eying an omnipotent adult, alert for some hint of his fate.

"Is that about the way it happened, David?" I finally asked.

"I—I guesso."

Nodding, I took a long, final moment to study him, then decided to say, "David, you're obviously a thoughtful, intelligent boy. And I imagine that you've already figured out why Inspector Canelli and I are questioning you about Sunday." I paused, then asked, "Have you figured it out?"

"I guesso." Now his eyes seemed to cling to mine, as if he were fearful of missing even the smallest change in my voice or my face.

"Why am I questioning you, then?"

"Because"—he gulped—"because you think that my—my uncle m—might—" He couldn't finish it. But, doggedly, he still stared directly into my eyes. The boy had courage—a silent, desperate, lonely courage that he himself probably didn't realize he possessed.

"If you were going to say," I replied, "that I think your uncle might've committed murder on Sunday, then I'd have to say that you're partly right and partly wrong."

"P—" He moistened his lips. "Partly wrong?"

I nodded. "What happened, you see, was that someone phoned into our office here and told us that we should talk to your uncle—ask him where he was on Sunday night. So, no matter how I felt about it, I *had* to talk to your uncle because I *had* to check out that phone call. It's one of the rules we work by. Do you understand?"

"But who would phone and say a—a thing like that? It—it's mean, to do something like that."

I shook my head. "It's not mean, David. You see, whoever phoned us was probably concerned that . . ."

"Didn't they even say who they were, whoever phoned?"

"No. It's what we call an anonymous tip. You've probably heard about—"

"But they *lied*. Whatever they said, they lied. My uncle is . . ." He twisted sharply to his right, meeting his mother's watchful gaze. "They lied," the boy repeated helplessly. "Whoever said it, they're a liar."

"You may be right, David," I said. "I hope, for your sake, that you are. But still, I have to check. Do you understand?"

Breathing rapidly, he turned away from his mother, twisting to face me fully. Now defiance smoldered in his soft, sad eyes.

"*Do* you understand?" I dropped my voice to a deeper, more authoritative note.

He nodded with slow, stubborn reluctance, small hands clenched into narrow, ineffectual fists—but still, clenched.

Ann would be pleased, I was thinking, if she could see David now.

"All right. Good. Now, what I particularly want to ask you is exactly what happened, minute by minute, from the time you arrived in the vicinity of Mr. Papa— of the popcorn wagon and the time you left for home." I paused briefly, deciding on the sequence of my questions. "First, do you remember whether the popcorn wagon was still parked there when you left the area?"

"N—no."

"Why not?" I dropped my voice another note.

"B—because we didn't leave that way. I mean, we just went off through the woods, like we usually do. We go more in the woods than on the sidewalks, usually."

"Why is that, David?"

"What?"

"Why do you walk mostly in the woods, you and your uncle?"

"Because it's more fun that way. I mean, it's like—" Glancing aside, suddenly embarrassed, he didn't finish it.

"It's more like cowboys and Indians—something like that. Is that what you were going to say?"

Looking with quick apprehension at his mother, as if he

feared her response, he shook his head. "No. We—we just walk in the woods. Away from people."

I decided to let the point go, at least for the moment. "You do things like watch squirrels, though."

Again looking at his mother, this time he nodded tentatively. Something in my last questions seemed to bother him.

"How many squirrels did you and your uncle see when you were in the area near the popcorn wagon?"

"We—we saw two. Just two."

"Did you follow them?"

"I—I don't know wh—what you mean."

"I mean that when you saw the squirrels, did you go after them? Maybe you followed one while your uncle followed the other."

Plainly, he now recognized the trap. I saw his body tense. His small fists tightened in his lap. "No. We watched them together. We were both together, all the time. Just like I told the— the other man. The fat one."

Dismayed, his mother caught her breath, looking at me with prim apology. Then she raised her eyes, elaborately despairing.

I hadn't smiled. "All right, David. Now I'd like to ask you something else. From what you and your uncle said, I gather that you arrived in the area in question—near the popcorn wagon, that is—sometime between four and five. And piecing it together, you probably remained in the area for a half-hour or so, most of which time you were in a wooded area close by, watching squirrels. We've already established all that, more or less. So now I'd like to ask you whether you saw anyone there— anyone that you knew, or recognized, or would remember if you saw again." As I said it, I slid open my center drawer, fingering the photograph of June Towers.

Licking his lips, he frowned. "Well, I saw the popcorn man. Is that what you mean?"

"Yes. Good. That's exactly what I mean. Who else?"

He looked away, concentrating. The odds were even, I realized, that he was calculating the effect of his testimony on the safety of his uncle.

76

"I—I saw some people," he answered finally. "But I didn't see anyone I knew, I don't think."

I slid the picture toward him. "Did you see this girl, David?"

He drew back, his eyes alarmed. "Th—that's the girl that was m—murdered."

I nodded. "That's right. June Towers. She was near you in the park on Sunday. Did you see her?"

Staring at the photograph, fascinated, his lips moved before the words came. "I didn't see her, though. Honest I didn't. And my uncle didn't see her, either. I *know* he didn't."

"Oh?" I pretended an offhand surprise. "He didn't see her?"

"N—no."

"How do you know he didn't, David?"

He slowly, painfully swallowed—giving himself time. "Because we—were together all the time," came the slow, stubborn answer. "So if I didn't see her, then James couldn't have, either."

"That's not necessarily true, David. Just because the two of you were together, that doesn't mean you were always looking in the same direction. Does it?"

His chin was beginning to quiver. Hastily, before the mother became alarmed at the boy's distress, I asked, "Did you see a green Volkswagen parked near the popcorn wagon, David?"

"N—no."

"Did you see a teen-aged boy on a motorcycle—a good-looking boy with blond hair, wearing a fringed leather jacket?"

A troubled silence. "Well," he said finally, "I could've, I guess. I mean, there're always lots of motorcycles around in the park."

"This teen-ager would've been parked, talking to someone in the green VW."

He hesitated. Then: "I—I don't think I did."

I described Lester Farley. He hadn't seen Farley, either. The boy was growing anxious again. Both the parents were plainly restive. My time was running out.

"How about a man in a white car, David? A white Ford, quite new."

He looked at me speculatively—as if I'd offered him something that he could perhaps accept. "I—I might've seen him." It was a timid reply, spoken in a low, uncertain voice—as if he were doubtful of his newly learned lines.

I nodded encouragement, saying, "Are you pretty good at telling cars apart, David?"

"Well—" He hesitated, worriedly blinking at me. "Well, maybe I'm not so good on all cars. But some I know."

"Do you think you could tell a Cadillac from, say, a Chevrolet?"

Frowning, clearly trying to visualize the two cars, he nodded slowly.

"How about a Chevrolet and a Ford?"

"I—I don't know. But I know a Mustang. And a Volkswagen. And a Buick, too. I can tell Buicks."

"What kind of a car do your parents have?"

"A Buick."

"All right. Now I'd like you to tell me about the man who was in this white car. What'd he look like?"

Biting his lips, he shook his head. "I—I can't—" He shook his head again, this time with a sudden, despairing sharpness.

"What color hair did he have? Dark or light?"

"Dark."

"About the color of mine?"

He examined my head with exaggerated care, then said, "Yes. Maybe a little more in front."

I smiled. "All right. Now what about his age?"

"Well, he was about your age, I guess."

"Not young and not old, then."

He nodded solemnly.

"Did he wear glasses?"

"No."

"What was he wearing? What kind of clothes?"

"I—I couldn't tell."

That much, at least, was true. As long as the man remained in the car, the clothing wouldn't have registered.

But was he telling the truth about the man in the white car?

Or was he merely seizing a last opportunity to turn suspicion away from his uncle?

I rose, extending my hand across the desk. "Thank you, David. You've been a lot of help. You're a bright boy and you're very loyal. I'll see you soon."

His grip, like his narrowly clenched fists, was too slight for a boy.

I turned to the mother. "I wonder whether you and David would mind waiting outside for a moment, Mrs. Fisher? I'd like to talk to your husband and you separately, to get adult verification of your son's testimony."

As she and the boy were leaving, my buzzer sounded. This time it was Markham.

"I've finally found the Miller kid—*not* in school."

"Where is he?"

"Here."

"Where?"

"Sitting at my desk. I'm talking from Culligan's phone."

"Keep him there. Start the interrogation. I'll be with you in twenty minutes."

"All right. Walter Cross is here, too."

Irritated, I tapped my pencil sharply on the desk. They'd all come at once. I had no one available to interrogate Cross. "Ask him to wait for a few minutes. At Canelli's desk. I'll have Canelli there as soon as possible."

"All right." The phone clicked dead.

I turned to Bill Fisher, smiling mechanically at him. "Sorry. A little administrative foul-up, I'm afraid."

With an obvious effort he returned the smile, shifting uncomfortably.

I settled back behind the desk, deliberately allowing a long, heavy silence to settle before saying, "I wish you'd take a few minutes and fill me in on your brother's background, Mr. Fisher."

Plainly, he was unprepared for the polite, placating tone in my voice, asking for his help, not demanding. If I'd chosen an opposite course, I felt, he would have met me head-on. Now, scrubbing his big-knuckled hand across the sparse fringe of his faded red hair, he looked at me uncertainly. "What'd you mean?" he asked with grudging civility.

I spread my hands. "I need to know everything I can about your brother. The more I know, the better."

"The better for who?"

"The better for him, if he's innocent. And for you, too."

"What kind of things do you want to know?"

"Start with his early life."

He snorted. But now his manner was more rueful than rude. "James was always a—an oddball. Always, even when he was a kid. He never had any friends. He never even tried to *make* any. He just—just moped around. Just exactly like he's doing right now."

"What was his profession?"

The other man shifted in his chair, flinging out his right hand in a flat, slicing movement. "He never had a profession. My—our—father was a painting contractor. He never had a big business, but it was always a good business. While James was in college, studying art and English and philosophy and everything, I was in Korea. Then my father died. I got out of the army, and came home, and took over the business. I knew James wouldn't be any good at it, so I told him to take his share of the insurance and stay in college. Which he did. When he finally got out of college—he never did graduate—he tried to be an artist for a while. Then he tried to write—poetry, for God's sake. But he could never do either one, and he could never hold any kind of a job that meant anything. And all the while he was getting—stranger."

"Did he live with you during that time?"

He shook his head abruptly. "No. He just lived—around. Half the time I didn't even know where he was living. Not until—" He broke off.

"Not until when?"

"Not until just before he got into that—that trouble. I hadn't seen him for two years—hadn't even heard from him for a year or more. Then he just showed up one day on our doorstep. He—

80

he looked like a bum, an honest-to-God bum." He shook his head again, baffled at the memory, angry. "We were living down in Redwood City then. We—we had a nice house in a nice neighborhood. I—I'd worked hard for years so that I could afford—" Again he broke off, staring down at my desk, blinking. "I guess you know the rest of it."

I nodded, asking, "How'd you happen to move to San Francisco?"

He shot me a resentful look. "The last couple of years, with this recession—" He shrugged irritably. "Where we're living now, that place belonged to my folks. We rented it out while we were in Redwood City. But last year we had to sell the house in Redwood City. Partly we needed money for the lawyer—James' lawyer. And partly it was the recession, like I said."

"So your present house is really half your brother's, I suppose."

He nodded, bobbing his head wearily.

"But you aren't really very happy with the arrangement," I pressed. "None of you."

"Not unless you count David, we aren't very happy. I might as well be honest about it."

I nodded, studying him as he sat hunched in the chair, his body oddly slack. "Do you have any idea who might've phoned us about your brother, Mr. Fisher?"

He shook his head. His wide chest heaved as he drew a deep breath.

"Do you think your brother killed June Towers?"

He raised his head. His voice was a ragged whisper as he said, "I don't know. I—I honest to God don't know."

"If your son is telling the truth, your brother can't be guilty."

His blank expression didn't change. He'd come to the end of his resources sooner than I'd expected. When the blustering was finished, so was Bill Fisher.

I dismissed him and asked him to send his wife in to me. During the interval I called the squad room, leaving instructions that Canelli was to finish with Randall Grant, then interview

Walter Cross. Grant was to wait for a few words with me. Later Cross was to do the same.

As I'd been talking on the phone, Marge Fisher came into the office and sat down directly across the desk from me. She looked as if she were a dissatisfied department-store customer come to complain about the service.

"I won't keep you but a moment, Mrs. Fisher," I said. "In fact, I don't have much time myself. I'd just like to ask you a few questions, if I may."

She sat with white-gloved hands holding her gleaming black handbag precisely centered in her lap. Her gaze was bright and hard, her face firmly set. Dressed in a checkered wool suit, her make-up applied with more precision than art, she suited perfectly the image of the middle-class housewife. Her previous night's wide-eyed uncertainty had vanished completely, along with her anxious apprehension for David just a few minutes before.

I decided to test her poise with a quick, tough question: "Do you think it's possible that your brother-in-law murdered the Towers girl, Mrs. Fisher?"

"I don't know, Lieutenant," she answered promptly. "It's your place to say, not mine. It's your job." Her voice was level, her eyes steady. She still seemed the brisk, hard-to-please department-store customer.

"That's true," I said. "But I'm asking for your opinion as to whether he's *capable* of murder. As a personality."

She paused briefly, considering. Finally, in a steady, measured voice, she said, "He almost committed murder two years ago. I don't think he's changed. If anything, he's worse."

"Psychologically, you mean."

"Yes."

"He's certainly on the ragged edge," I agreed. "At least as far as I can see." I paused. Then, still with my voice at a casual, neutral pitch, I asked, "Do you mind your son seeing so much of James?"

The white gloves tightened spasmodically on the black purse.

82

"Yes, Lieutenant, I *do* mind. Very much." Her voice was unnaturally soft, her eyes unnaturally bright.

"I can understand that. By the way, do you have any idea who might've phoned us about your brother-in-law?"

She drew a deep, measured breath. "No, I don't. But I can tell you it could've been lots of people—a half-dozen, for instance, right on our block."

"Why do you say that?"

"Because it's the truth. People don't like the idea of a—a criminal living next door."

"Does he go outside much—mix with the neighbors?"

"No," she answered slowly, making an obvious effort at quiet, ladylike self-control. "No, he doesn't go out much, except with David. But people come in, you know. And people talk. Believe me," she said softly, her outraged eyes straying off, "people talk."

"I can imagine. It must be very difficult for you."

She made no reply, but instead modestly dropped her gaze to the gleaming black plastic handbag, sighing faintly.

"As to whether your brother-in-law is actually guilty of the Towers murder," I said, "that, of course, depends on whether or not your son's testimony is accurate—whether it would stand up in court, for instance." I paused, then asked quietly, "What do you think, Mrs. Fisher? Is his testimony accurate?"

She still sat bowed over the handbag. When she raised her head, her expression for the first time seemed hesitant, unsure. Finally, with plain reluctance, she said, "Two years ago, in the judge's chambers, David gave some testimony that—hurt James's chances. I tried not to let David know. We never really talked about it, but I've always thought that he *did* know. So now—" She gestured with her gloved hand: a small, eloquently regretful raising of the fingers. "Now he'd rather die, he thinks, than do anything to hurt his uncle. But"—she licked at her lips—"but the truth is that last night David let it slip that during their walk yesterday he and James played hide-and-seek. It came out because David mentioned what a good hiding place James must've found. He couldn't find his uncle for a long time, he said. So

I—" Her voice caught. Eyes averted, she swallowed painfully before saying softly, "It isn't that David was lying. It's just that— that he couldn't tell it all."

"Was it near the scene of the crime that they played hide-and-seek?" As I asked the question, I became aware that I suddenly felt very tired.

"I think so. But I—I'm not sure."

"Do you realize what you're saying, Mrs. Fisher?"

She nodded slowly.

I sat for a long moment staring at her bowed head. Then: "I'd like you and your husband to wait in the reception room for a few minutes. Fifteen minutes, say. Will you do that?"

She nodded, rose, and left my office. She didn't look at me directly.

Thirteen

Friedman gestured for a patrolman to keep watch at his open office door, then walked with me to an empty interrogation room. "You first," he said.

Conscious of Randall Grant, Kent Miller, and Walter Cross, all waiting for me, I outlined the Fisher interrogation as quickly and concisely as possible. No matter what we decided to do with James Fisher, I still wanted to talk to the other subjects.

When I'd finished, Friedman snorted ruefully. "Hide-and-seek. Jesus. I can't even remember how the game goes."

I glanced at my watch. "What'd you think? Shall we hold him?"

"If we lock that character up now," Friedman said, "I can promise you one thing for sure: by morning, we'll have a gibbering idiot on our hands."

"I know."

"I've got to admit, though," he said, "that it's been an experience interrogating him—something like listening to the sound track of a Dali painting. By the way, have you seen the afternoon papers?"

"No."

85

"They've got the whole story on James Fisher—his record in San Mateo, his brother's business, everything. I couldn't believe it."

"I suppose," I said, "that I should interrogate the kid again. If his testimony stands up, the uncle's clean."

"And if the mother's stands up, the uncle's screwed."

I nodded.

"You know," he said reflectively, "it's almost as if Marge Fisher wants to nail the uncle—who just happens to be her kid's best friend, apparently. Or maybe his only friend."

I realized that something Ann had said last night was nagging at a remote corner of my consciousness. We'd been in bed. And she'd . . .

"You look like you've lost your last friend, as my father used to say," Friedman said.

"I guess I'm not very fond of questioning loonies and kids."

He looked at me thoughtfully before saying, "Why don't you talk to Grant, Miller and company. I'll finish with the uncle, then talk to the kid and his parents. I'll see what I think, and we can compare notes."

"Assuming the kid confirms his mother's testimony, do you think we should let the uncle go home?"

Friedman shrugged. "He's not going anywhere, Frank. He might hide in his potting shed, or in some dark closet. But he's sure as hell not going anywhere."

"Potting shed?"

"Didn't he tell you about the potting shed?"

"No."

"That's where he and the kid spend most of their time, when they aren't playing hide-and-seek in the park. It's their clubhouse, I gather. Just before you knocked, James was telling me how he responds to plants and how plants respond to him."

I stepped to the door. "You're probably right, about him not going anywhere. I'll see you later. If I'm not available, and you decide to release him, go ahead. The more I think about it, the more I think maybe we should contact the D.A.'s office before we book him."

"Why would you want to do a silly thing like that?" Friedman's long-suffering relationship with the D.A.'s office was a departmental saga.

"Because," I answered, "we've got a contradiction—a crucial contradiction—between a minor's testimony and his parent's, quoting him. Personally, I think it's a legal question. Unless we get the D.A.'s opinion, I think we could lose either way we jump."

"Nonsense, Lieutenant. You're getting bogged down in legalities. Good investigators need flair—imagination. The light touch. You go about your lower-level interrogations and leave the Fishers to me. The entire Fishers." He clapped me hard on the shoulder, propelling me toward the door.

Fourteen

I found Randall Grant fidgeting in the waiting room. He was dressed in a conservative double-knit suit, paisley-printed tie, gleaming cuffs, and highly polished black shoes. His dark hair was carefully combed, lotioned to a glossy gigolo sheen.

I apologized for keeping him waiting and took him down the corridor to my office. As he sat facing me, he flicked back his cuff to glance at an elaborate gold wristwatch. All of his movements seemed carefully planned. He was a heavy-moving man, heavily handsome.

"I'll just take a few minutes of your time, Mr. Grant. I didn't get a chance to talk to you yesterday. And besides, it wasn't the right time."

He shrugged indifferently, kneading the flesh beneath his jaw with thumb and forefinger as he looked at me with dark, opaque eyes.

"According to what your wife said yesterday," I began, "you're having, ah, marital difficulties."

He said, "Everyone I know has marital difficulties." His low, coarse voice was uninflected.

"That's not an answer," I said, making it official.

He snorted. "So okay. We're having problems. And yeah, we're going to get divorced. So it's no big deal. It's happened to both of us before."

"What's your line of work, Mr. Grant?"

"I'm in real estate."

"A salesman?"

He shook his head insolently, challenging me with his agate eyes. "No, I'm not a salesman. I'm a broker. I've been a broker for five years."

"What did you do before you sold real estate?"

"I sold cars. Lots of cars."

I nodded. "By the way, what kind of a car do you drive, Mr. Grant?"

"A Cad."

"Is it white?"

"No, it's green, as a matter of fact. Dark metallic-green. Why?"

I allowed a deliberate moment to pass before saying softly, "No reason. Just checking." But my manner was calculated to contradict my words.

His dark, heavy eyebrows almost met as he frowned at me. Drawing himself up straighter in the chair, hunching his shoulders to adjust his jacket as he leaned forward, he said, "Say, what's with the car—the white car? The other one—Canelli— asked the same thing. What're you getting at, anyhow?"

Knowing that it would aggravate him further, I ignored the question. "It occurs to me," I said, "that you're a good person to give us an unbiased evaluation of the victim."

Again he snorted. "What's *that* supposed to mean, anyhow?"

"It means that I'd like you to tell me what kind of a girl June Towers really was."

"Well, why ask me?" As he said it, his scowling, self-confidence seemed to falter, revealing a tiny, almost imperceptible tic of doubt. As I watched his eyes shift slightly, I realized that I'd struck a nerve. Unwittingly.

"Tell me about June Towers, Mr. Grant," I said quietly.

"That's why you're here—to tell me about her." I settled back as if I had the whole afternoon.

The tic was more obvious now. The fingers were tighter. The chin was uneasily upthrust, loosening the thick, sallow neck inside the immaculate collar. As he shifted impatiently in the chair and jerkily resettled himself, he glanced at me with a fleeting, oblique appraisal. "What's she been saying, anyhow?" he demanded.

"Your wife, you mean." Taking a gambler's chance, I inflected it as a flat statement, not a question.

Suddenly he was no longer the smooth-moving, barroom-handsome Cad-owner. Leaning farther forward, ready to make a hustler's deal, his eyes were avid, his mouth slightly upcurved, thinly ingratiating. I caught an almost inaudible whine in his voice as he said, "Whatever she said, she was just repeating what the kid told her. And—hell—what could I say? I just took it and grinned, that's all. I'd had it. I decided to get out, right then. And that's exactly what I'm doing—getting out. Christ, between the two of them, what chance did I have?"

"Why don't you tell me about it," I said softly. "Give me your version. Let's see how they compare."

"Sure. Great. But what the hell is my word worth, now that June's dead? Ellen can say anything she wants."

"What other choice do you have, though?"

He licked his full lips, stared at me for a long, calculating moment, then sighed, elaborately resigned. He was prepared to pitch me.

"I guess you're right, at that." He paused a last time before saying, "First of all, I admit that I was gassed. Ellen had to fly up to her sister's that night, like she probably told you. In Seattle. So I went out, ah, bar-hopping. But I was home at one, or maybe a little after. I was gassed, like I said. I was having a nightcap and watching the late movie up in our room. And I heard June come in. She'd been out with the Miller kid, which I knew. And I heard her downstairs, in the refrigerator. So pretty soon she comes upstairs. And then she comes in the room—to watch the movie, she says. Real cool. That's how she was—real cool. Just the way she moved, you knew that she was—"

He paused, lost in thought, his eyes unfocused, momentarily back in the past. Finally, collecting himself, he went on in a deeper, more impersonal voice. "Anyhow, I was lying on the bed, with a drink, watching the movie. I was dressed, and everything—just lying on the spread. So she—she got on the bed, too, so she could watch the movie, she said. And I knew, right then, that she'd probably had a couple of drinks herself. Or maybe she'd smoked pot, or taken something else. I don't know. The only thing I know is that she dropped her coat on the floor and crawled across the bed—it's king size—and she was lying propped up against the headboard, right next to me, watching the goddamn TV. And—" He shook his head sharply, as if stung by a sudden pain. "And hell, she was wearing a goddamn sweater, like they all wear, and tight pants. And then, the next thing I know, her shoulder's touching me, and her leg. And then—well—" He licked at his lips. Remembering the moment, his eyes were moist, his breathing quicker. "And then—Christ—the next thing I know, I—I'm touching her. And I'll admit it, I—I couldn't keep my hands off her. And before I know it, she's got her clothes off, and she's really—really putting it to me. And Christ, I'm going along with it. I mean, I'm only human, and if you saw her, you know she was—was—" He was muttering now, almost incoherent.

"She was really built. Is that what you were going to say?"

His head fell forward. He'd suddenly gone slack. His eyes were blank, his mouth hung slightly open. He sat round-shouldered, hunched over, staring sightlessly at the floor.

"So you made love to her."

His head jerked up. *"No.* Christ, *no,* I didn't. I—I don't deny that I wanted to. I—I had about half my clothes off, and was all ready to go, when all of a sudden—just in a flash—I realized what the hell I was doing. Like, statutory rape. A friend of mine got nailed on that, and he got nailed good. So just at the last second I rolled away. I swear to God, I rolled off that bed and I got dressed."

91

"And what did she . . ." My buzzer sounded. Masking my annoyance, I answered.

"It's Canelli, Lieutenant. I'm sorry to bother you, because I already know you're with the Grant guy. But that's what I wanted to tell you: something's bothering him, about the girl. I couldn't get at it, quite, but I felt like I was getting close when I had to take Cross. But I thought you ought to know that . . ."

"Right. I'll see you in fifteen minutes or so."

"Oh. Yeah. Right. Goodbye, Lieutenant. Good luck."

I hung up, turning to Grant. He was lighting a cigarette. His fingers were steady. I'd probably lost him.

Pushing an ashtray across the desk, I asked softly, "What did she do, Mr. Grant, while you were dressing?"

"She started swearing at me. I mean, she started swearing like a whore who hadn't got paid. She laid there on the bed, naked, looking up at me and swearing in a kind of a—a low, vicious way, like she'd like to see me dead. It—it shook me up. It really did. Then she said I'd pay. 'You'll pay, you son of a bitch,' she kept saying."

"And did you?"

"How'd you mean?"

"I mean, did you pay? With money, for instance?"

He nodded, stubbing out his half-smoked cigarette. "Yeah," he said heavily. "I paid. Not much, but I paid."

"How much, would you say?"

He shrugged. "I don't know. I didn't keep track. She'd be going out shopping, or something, and if she could get me alone, she'd say, 'Give me ten, you bastard.' Or, 'Give me twenty.'"

"Did you give it to her?"

"Sometimes. It depended."

"How long ago did this incident take place?"

"Five, six months ago."

"And eventually she told her mother. Is that it?"

"She told her mother that I *screwed* her, that's what she told her mother. Christ—" He looked at me with baffled eyes. "Christ, I thought that's what this was all about. I thought that Ellen must've said that . . ." He broke off, then began to mutter

92

a long string of dull, listless obscenities. Finally he said, "You can't win with the goddamn broads. You just can't win."

"Where were you between the hours of four P.M. and eight P.M. on Sunday evening, Mr. Grant?" I said sharply.

He spat out a last obscenity. "I was at home. All night. What'd that bitch say? That I wasn't, or something? Is that what she said?"

I rose. "I'd like you to wait for me in the waiting room. Where you were when I found you." I walked around the desk and opened the door. He left without speaking to me, shoulders hunched, still muttering to himself. Cad-owners, I was thinking, deflated quickly.

I detailed a patrolman to keep an unobtrusive eye on Grant, then instructed Canelli to bring Walter Cross to my office in ten minutes. I next phoned the Grant home, only to be told by a helpful neighbor that Mrs. Grant was at the undertaker's.

Fifteen

Remembering him as I'd seen him yesterday, and seeing him now, Walter Cross looked like an actor who'd disappeared through his dressing-room door made up for a down-at-the-heels character role and emerged as a leading man. He was neatly dressed and clean-shaven, with his hair cut modishly long and carefully combed in graceful waves. He was completely at home in his expensive suit. Plainly, the feel of good clothes was important to him. He sat in my visitor's chair, elegantly flicking at his trouser-creases as he crossed his legs, and I realized that his finely drawn, poetic good looks would probably have great appeal for a certain kind of sensitive, insecure woman. Watching him, I thought of an old Leslie Howard–Bette Davis movie I'd recently seen on TV. But I couldn't remember the title.

"You look a hundred percent better," I said. "I hope you feel as well as you look."

"I had a good breakfast. Ham and eggs. It helps," he admitted.

"Good." I nodded at him, smiling slightly. "I won't take much of your time, Mr. Cross. Mainly I wanted to ask you whether you'd thought of anything that might help us with any back-

94

ground information on June Towers." As I was speaking, I realized that the question was meaningless—bland, pointless. I was still preoccupied with thoughts of Randall Grant, suddenly a suspect. Grant had a motive, and his relationship with the victim could account for the hidden three hundred dollars. He was probably a hothead, probably capable of violence. He could even have an arrest record—something I should have checked.

But Randall Grant also had an alibi: his wife, soon to be his ex-wife—therefore, all the more compelling as a witness. Their undisguised hatred for each other could actually strengthen Grant's case.

". . . told you everything I could yesterday, Lieutenant," Cross was saying. "I really don't see what I can add."

Collecting myself, focusing on him, I said, "Did she ever talk to you about her home life? Did she ever mention her mother—or her stepfather?"

He sighed, languidly patient. "As I said yesterday, Lieutenant, I actually had practically nothing to do with the girl. Even after my wife was—gone, and June spent more time with Steffie and myself, I actually talked to her very little. She and Steffie were always together, chattering away in Steffie's room. Which, of course, was wonderful for Steffie. She—" Suddenly, talking of his stepdaughter, pain shadowed his eyes. He winced momentarily, looking away. Then, in a subdued voice, he said, "June was a very quiet girl, Lieutenant. Very quiet. Very—self-contained. I just—" He shrugged. "I just didn't know much about her."

"She might've been quiet," I said, "but the information we're getting indicates that she wasn't exactly demure. Do you have any comment on that?"

"No," he said, "I don't. But then I imagine that 'demure' these days is a matter of interpretation."

"I suppose you're right." I hesitated, carefully framing my next question: "For some time," I said, "June Towers was, in a sense, part of your family. You saw her every day. She spent a lot of time with you. Is that right?"

Frowning slightly, as if I'd puzzled him, he said, "Yes, that's right. That's what I told you yesterday."

"I know you did. And I realize that you were so preoccupied with your wife's problems that June didn't really register on you as a person. Still, you must've had some idea of her character."

"I think I've already told you—she was quiet. She said very little. She always did her job."

"Was she punctual?"

"Usually, yes."

"Was she honest?"

"Yes."

"Was she ever insolent?"

"No. Never."

I paused, then in an offhand voice I said, "Did she ever make —advances to you, Mr. Cross?"

He was obviously perplexed. "Advances?"

I nodded. "Sexual advances."

He snickered, shaking his head, smiling ruefully. "No, Lieutenant. She never tried to seduce me. It would have been a—a welcome experience, I don't mind admitting. She was a good-looking girl. But she never tried. And I didn't try either, if that's the next question."

"No, Mr. Cross," I answered, "that wasn't the next question. I did want to ask you, though, for the name and residence of your wife's parents."

"Why do you want to know that?"

"Just as a matter of information. Your stepdaughter spent a lot of time with the victim. Her testimony could help us."

"You mean that you want to interview Steffie?" He asked the question incredulously.

"Yes."

"But"—he swallowed, licking at his lips—"but Steffie's just a girl—a little girl."

"Sometimes children know more than they think they do, Mr. Cross."

"Yes. I—I see what you mean." Obviously troubled, he eyed

me uneasily. Finally he muttered, "The name is Platt. Charles Platt. They live on Pacific Avenue, here in the city."

"Good. Thanks." I watched him squirm for a moment, then pushed myself back from the desk. "By the way, what kind of a car do you drive?"

"A Ford."

Rounding my desk, I paused. I was conscious of a small swelling of visceral excitement. "What year Ford?"

"Last year's," he answered uneasily. "Why?"

"What's the color, Mr. Cross?"

"It's red. Actually red and black. A hard top."

The slight swell of excitement slowly subsided. "Were you at home Sunday evening?" I asked casually.

He dropped his eyes, shame-faced. Standing facing me, he seemed less sure of himself—less comfortable in his beautifully fitting clothes. "I haven't gone out evenings for—for months," he answered in a low voice.

"Actually, I should've said Sunday afternoon."

With an obvious effort he raised his head, searching my face with anxious eyes. "Th—that's when June was—was murdered."

"We have a report of a dark-haired, middle-aged man at the murder scene, Mr. Cross—driving a white Ford. So, naturally, we're checking out anyone associated with the victim who answers that description."

As his eyes still searched my face, I saw his urbane, leading-man's face begin to pull itself apart, revealing the haggard, hollow-eyed mask of twitching failure that I'd first seen yesterday.

"I was home Sunday," he finally managed. "All day. I didn't go out except for a—a short trip to the corner, for a bottle. Y—you can check with my neighbors. They'll tell you. Ev—every step I take, down to the corner and back, I can feel them watching me. Every single step."

I opened the door. "Thanks for coming down, Mr. Cross. I hope you find a decorating client soon."

He tried to smile, jerkily extending his hand. His grip was weak. "I hope so, too, Lieutenant. I—" He gulped suddenly, and turned abruptly away, striking the doorframe with his shoulder as he left. Watching the door close, I wondered how long it would take him to buy a bottle and get back to his dark, musty living room.

I turned to the desk and dialed Friedman.

"I've just released all the Fishers," he said immediately. "The whole crew. Much as I hate to admit it, I think we might have to set up a conference with the D.A. What happened with you?"

I recounted the Randall Grant interrogation and was rewarded by a long, low whistle. "That's pretty fair interrogating, Lieutenant. Pretty fair indeed. Now, if we can just trap the wife into admitting that Grant went out for cigarettes, or something, we'll have a brand-new suspect."

"Why don't you take Markham and go out and see her? I'll keep the husband here until I hear from you. I've still got to question Kent Miller, too. He's with Markham now, waiting for me."

I heard him sigh. Friedman freely admitted a preference for the comfort of the office.

"All right." He paused, then said, "You know, that Fisher woman is a real sugar-lipped bitch. I'll bet you a three-dollar lunch that she's the anonymous tipster."

"Maybe."

I could hear Friedman heaving himself to his feet. "Okay, I'm off. I'll check with you later. Anything else?"

"Walter Cross seemed jumpy, especially when I told him that I was going to interview his stepdaughter."

"All the more reason to have her interrogated, then."

"I'll send Culligan out on it."

Sixteen

Catching Markham's eye across the almost-deserted inspectors' room, I beckoned to him. He left Kent Miller seated at his desk and came toward me, walking leisurely, adjusting his tie. His eyes were expressionless, his mouth unsmiling. He moved with the smooth, deliberate gait of a predator, always alert.

"Well," I asked, seating myself on a desk-corner, "how'd it go?"

"I think," he said flatly, "that something's bugging him. Badly."

"Did he see her in the park? On his motorcycle?"

"He won't admit it. He won't admit anything. But I think he saw her. He's got a fringed leather jacket, too."

"I'll talk to him. Anything else I should know?"

"Not really."

"Where're his folks?"

"Working."

"Was he at home when you found him?"

"Yes. 'Sick,' he said. I'll give him that, anyhow. He *looked* sick."

"He came downtown of his own free will, though."

His only reply was a long-suffering nod.

"All right—" I rose from the desk. "Lieutenant Friedman is waiting for you in his office. He'll fill you in." I turned away, walking to Markham's desk.

"Hello, Kent," I said quietly. "How's it going today?"

His shoulders moved in a slow, languidly expressive adolescent shrug, conveying both defiance and dismay—both uneasiness and indifference. At his elbow was an ashtray. He was moodily stirring a half-dozen cigarette butts with a not-quite-clean forefinger. He didn't raise his eyes.

Something, certainly, was bugging him.

"I had the feeling yesterday," I began, "that we were just getting to something important when I had to leave. That's why I wanted you to come down today."

Again he shrugged, then nodded. "Yeah. Sure." With an obvious effort, he turned away from the ashtray. His forehead and upper lip were perspiration-beaded. Now he slowly raised his left hand to his mouth, nibbling at the thumbnail.

"I especially wanted to ask you again whether you saw June at any time on Sunday," I said. "Any time at all—morning or evening."

For a moment he didn't reply. Then, taking his hand down from his mouth, he mumbled, "I just talked to her on the phone. Like I told you."

"You didn't actually *see* her?"

"No. I *told* you." His voice slipped into a higher note, aggrieved.

"I just wanted to make sure, Kent. That's what police work is, you know: double-checking, then double-checking again."

He didn't reply.

"I also wanted to ask you about what you actually did Sunday —after, say, you talked to June on the phone. That was about—" I paused, faking a puzzled frown. "When did you say it was that you talked to her?"

"A—about three."

"Right. Thanks. And you said, I remember, that you were working on your motorcycle."

He nodded doggedly.

100

"Was it after you talked to June, or before, that you were working on your motorcycle?"

"Before *and* after."

"And you said that you rode your motorcycle on Sunday. When was that?"

"W—what'd you mean?"

"I mean, when did you ride your motorcyle on Sunday—at what time of the day?"

"Well, I—I rode it all day, off and on. I—I was trying to fix the carburetor. And all day long I was testing it out."

"Were you riding it at about five o'clock?"

"I—I don't remember. Maybe."

"Did you ride it in the park when you were testing it?"

"Once or twice."

I sat silently, watching him, letting him squirm. Finally, very quietly, I asked, "Did you ride it in the park between four o'clock and six, Kent?"

He shook his head sharply, suddenly turning half away from me. He was blinking rapidly. His lower lip was trembling. "How should I know?" he blurted plaintively. "Christ, I don't keep track of every little minute when I'm riding the bike."

Still speaking quietly, I said, "What I really want to know, Kent—what I've *got* to know—is whether, at any time on Sunday, you saw June Towers in the park. Because we have information that she was seen talking to someone who answers your description. Right down to the fringed leather jacket."

He suddenly twisted to face me, for the first time looking at me squarely. His eyes were wide, his throat painfully corded. Behind drawn-back lips, his teeth were tightly clenched. His voice was a low, strangled whisper. "Are you trying to say that I had something to do with killing her? Is that what you're trying to say?" As he spoke, a single tear streaked each cheek. His eyes were brimming. His voice was unsteady, about to break. "Because if—if you are, you—" He broke off. He was snuffling now, breathing through his mouth. His chest was heaving.

"All I want to know, Kent, is whether you saw her Sunday. That's all I . . ."

101

"You have to give me a lawyer. You can't do this. Last night my dad told me that—that—" He turned away, his eyes seeking the door.

"I just want an answer, Kent. No one's accusing you of anything. I just want to know whether . . ."

"All *right,* then. I *saw* her. For a second—a minute—I saw her. I—I didn't even know she was *there.* And I—I—" Shaking his head violently, he sprang to his feet, standing with fists clenched, mouth working. He looked like a child about to throw a tantrum.

It was time to back off. Legally, I'd already gone too far.

"No one's suggesting you're implicated in her murder, Kent. That's not the point. The point is that first you told us one thing, then you told us another. You said you didn't see her. Then you . . ."

"But I—I—"

"You go home now. Get some rest, and talk to your parents when they get home. We'll see you later."

He blinked, wiping at his nose with the back of his hand. He glanced furtively around the room to see whether anyone had noticed his tears. He seemed irresolute—surprised at my response. "Y—you want me to—to go home?"

"Yes. As I say, we'll be talking to you later. With your parents."

He frowned, biting at his lips, still confused.

"We'll see you tonight probably," I repeated. "If you'll wait outside in the waiting room, I'll have someone take you home."

Mumbling vague, garbled thanks, he stumbled toward the door. I called Canelli and told him to drive Kent Miller home, watch the house for a half-hour, concealed, then report back to the office.

Seventeen

I was in the cafeteria, eating a sandwich, when I saw Canelli standing in the doorway. Smiling sheepishly, half saluting, he made his shambling way toward me, clattering against a half-dozen chairs.

"Sit down."

"Thanks, Lieutenant." He placed his misshapen hat beside my coffee cup. It was Friedman's theory that to keep the underworld guessing, Canelli crushed his hat differently every day.

"Did Kent Miller stay home?"

"Yep."

"Did he say anything to you?"

"No. But I didn't push him." He glanced at me questioningly. "Was that right?"

I nodded. "Exactly right. Coffee?"

"No, thanks. Say, did you know that Lester Farley is here?"

"What's he want?"

"I think he has some information for you. Anyhow, he won't talk to me. I thought you knew he was here."

"No," I said, "I didn't know. Bring him upstairs in fifteen minutes. I'd like to talk to him."

"Okay. How's the case going, anyhow? It seems like everything is happening at once."

"Everything and nothing. We'll know more when we see what Ellen Grant says."

"I saw her husband in the waiting room. He's really fuming."

"As soon as I hear from Lieutenant Friedman, I'll let him go."

"You know," Canelli said slowly, his mouth twisted into an expression of deep concentration, "it seems to me that a lot depends on why June Towers was where she was. Know what I mean?"

"Not exactly."

"Well, we've been figuring that she just stopped at that particular place in the park for no real reason—because she just happened to be there, maybe to buy some popcorn, or something. But I been thinking that maybe she was there on purpose. And I've also been thinking that maybe the Miller kid knew *why* she was there."

"Did he say anything that led you to think that?"

"No, it's just a feeling I have."

"Well, you could be right. But still, she left her house mad. Which doesn't seem to indicate any previous plans to meet anyone at any particular time."

"I know. But I was thinking that. . ."

"Lieutenant Hastings." It was a busboy's voice, behind me. "Telephone. At the cashier's stand."

"Thanks." And to Canelli: "Wait for me."

It was Friedman, phoning from a drugstore in the Grants' neighborhood.

"We might have something," he said. "I don't know. I can't figure it."

"What happened?"

"Well, the facts are that Randall Grant and his wife apparently kept on arguing after the girl slammed out. The argument got hotter, until finally Mrs. Grant slammed out, too. That was about five o'clock. Maybe a little before. She had to get some cigarettes, she said, which she got at a neighborhood bar. She

104

got the cigarettes and decided to have a couple of drinks. Stingers. Then she went back home—apparently refueled and ready to start arguing again."

"Was Grant there when she got back?"

"Yes."

"Was it dark?"

"Yes."

"Did she have any idea why you were interrogating her?"

"As soon as I started," he said slowly, "she knew something was up. She was on her guard. At first I didn't get the significance of it. But finally it dawned on me."

"*What* dawned on you?"

"That she was worried. But not for hubby."

"For herself, you mean."

"Exactly. She was very careful to point out that all her time away from home was accounted for—a hundred and ten percent. Which isn't, I submit, the standard attitude of the grieving mother. I mean, under ordinary circumstances it wouldn't even occur to her that she needed to account for her time. It was almost as if she expected to be questioned—as if she was scared of what her husband had told us, instead of vice versa."

Glancing at the avidly listening cashier, I asked Friedman to hang on while I hurried to my office, closing the door behind me.

"That was a quick trip," Friedman said. "But then, you're a jogger."

"Go ahead."

"Well, as far as the mother is concerned, if you don't count conjecture, there really isn't much more to tell—beyond the obvious fact that neither she nor her husband has an alibi for the time of the murder. Not at this point, anyhow—not until we check out the neighbors and the bartender and God knows who."

"Do you actually think it's possible that she could've killed her own daughter?"

He hesitated, finally saying, "I don't know, Frank. I really don't know. But you know the old saying: most murder victims

105

either raised their murderer or else were raised *with* them. Or, in this case, maybe *by* them. Which, I admit, is a little rare."

"But this isn't a typical domestic homicide M.O. Usually they pick up a butcher knife, or a paperweight, and that's that. No premeditation. Besides, what's the motive?"

"Jealousy."

"I don't believe it."

"Don't get off on the wrong foot, Lieutenant. You're assuming an old-fashioned scenario: stepfather makes out with stepdaughter. Mother is outraged, slices up husband. But give your imagination a little exercise. This is the age of the pill, remember—the mother-and-daughter pill."

"You're saying that the mother and daughter were in competition for Randall Grant."

"Precisely. And maybe the mother was coming off second best. Personally, I don't believe Randall Grant rolled off that bed. I think he rolled the other way."

"So the mother went out for cigarettes. She had a couple of drinks. Whereupon she got in her car and met her daughter and killed her. With a blunt instrument." I shook my head.

"You're oversimplifying, old son. You're getting emotional. Furthermore, you're assuming that . . ."

"How would she know where to find the girl?"

"That," he replied, "is what we don't know. In fact, we have only a very hazy idea why June Towers was where she was, *when* she was. And it's my theory that when we do a little digging in that particular boneyard, we'll know a lot more than we do now."

"Canelli was just saying the same thing," I said.

"For once, Canelli and I agree."

"Did you ask Ellen Grant whether she knew about June's relations with Randall—assuming there actually were any relations?"

"No," he answered slowly, "I didn't."

"Why not?"

"Because I got so intrigued with her elaborately constructed

106

system of self-defenses that I didn't want to interrupt her. Besides, based on what you said, I figured she already knew."

"Yes, but which version did she have—her daughter's or her husband's?"

"What's the difference?" His voice was bland. I could visualize Friedman's expression: professorial, supremely self-satisfied. Normally, concocting his theories, he liked to hold forth in the squad room, lolling belly-up in an inspector's chair, airily examining his cigar ash as he talked, holding amiable court.

"There's a *lot* of difference. One way, the mother gets the story approximately the way Grant told it to me. He's the innocent party who finally flops off the bed. But the other way, sure as hell, she'd get it that he tried to screw June, and didn't make it. I have never—repeat, *never*—known a woman, young or old, to admit that she tried to seduce a man and failed."

"Now, now. Don't get overwrought. You're losing sight of the main point."

"What point is that?"

"Very simply that we have probably accounted for June's mysterious stash of money. We also have a motive—either for the father or the mother. Now all we need to know is . . ."

"Father *or* mother?" I interrupted sarcastically. "Don't you have a favorite?"

"We can discuss that later. This phone booth is too cramped to support any really creative thought. This is just an outline, so to speak."

"Oh. Of course."

"What I would like to have you do, Lieutenant, is release Randall Grant forthwith. Tell him to go home. I'll give him a half-hour or so, and then Markham and I will burst in on them. We'll separate them and see what happens. Which will, I predict, be plenty."

"But . . ."

"Meanwhile, I think that you and Canelli should reinterrogate Kent Miller, after he's had time to stew a little."

"I'd planned to. This evening."

"Excellent. We still have to figure out how the murderer knew June Towers was at that precise place at that precise time. And I figure that Kent Miller knows."

I drew a deep breath. "You might be right."

"I've been right before. About thirty-five percent of the time, in fact, I'm right. This could be one of those times."

"All right. I'll get Grant on his way. Then I want to spend a few minutes talking to Lester Farley, who's downstairs."

"What's Farley doing there?"

"Canelli says he has some information for me."

"How did Culligan come out with Cross's stepdaughter?"

"She's in Hawaii, with her grandmother. They won't be back until tomorrow or the next day."

"Well, good luck with Farley."

"Thanks."

Eighteen

"Sit down, Mr. Farley." I gestured to my visitor's chair.

"Thank you."

He sat with knees together, hands clasped in his lap. He wore exactly the same clothing he'd worn yesterday. His hair was carefully combed, his glasses sparkled. His pale, narrow face seemed anxiously drawn. Watching him as he cleared his throat, settling himself in the chair with nervous little rump-twitches, I tried to imagine him as a child setting cats on fire.

"Have you thought of anything else that might help us?" As I asked the question I glanced at my watch. At the most, I had ten minutes for Lester Farley.

"But—" He frowned. "But I thought you'd already arrested someone. Tha—" He moistened his lips. "That's what I wanted to tell you—that I remembered seeing the man and the boy on Sunday. The ones in the newspaper stories."

"Do you remember seeing anyone else?"

"Besides the man and the boy, you mean?"

I nodded.

"Well, as a matter of fact," he said slowly, "I spent a lot of

109

time thinking about it yesterday. I talked with Mother about it, too. Mother's very interested in psychic phenomena."

He paused, as if he expected some response. I murmured inarticulate encouragement, at the same time glancing pointedly at my watch.

"Last night," he continued, in the same slow, solemn voice, "we tried an experiment."

Counterfeiting an interest I didn't feel, I leaned forward. "What kind of an experiment, Mr. Farley?"

"Well, Mother had me lay down on the couch and close my eyes. She said she was going to guide me back to Sunday evening, so that I could remember everything I saw in the park. And it worked." He nodded primly, his faced puckered in an earnest frown. "It really worked. I went into a kind of a—a trance. And I could remember it all. Everything."

"Tell me about it. Tell me in sequence—just the way you remember it."

"Yes. Well—" As he drew a long, deep breath, his eyes lost focus. His voice changed to a softer, more remote pitch. "Well, I remember that I was walking along the sidewalk. I remember thinking that it would be dark soon. Dark and cold. And just about then I saw the popcorn wagon. I was walking from Kennedy Drive toward Fulton, going home. Because on Sundays, you see, we always have dinner earlier. We have a late breakfast and no lunch. Then we have an early dinner. So—" He frowned, hesitating. He'd lost the thread. I decided to remain silent, simply watching. And finally he nodded, brightening. He said, "So then, just as I got to the popcorn wagon, I saw the girl. She was in her car—her little green car. And I saw the man and the boy, too."

"What were the man and the boy doing?"

"They were up toward the trees. They were just—" He frowned. "Just there."

"All right. What happened then?"

"Well, the girl got out of her car and walked toward the popcorn wagon. And the woman was walking toward her."

"The woman?"

110

"Yes."

"Did the vic—did June Towers talk to this woman?"

"Yes."

"Did they know each other, would you say?"

"I—I think so." He hesitated. "But I don't think they liked each other."

"Was the woman older than the victim?"

"Yes."

"Do you think you could identify this woman if you were to see her again?"

He drew a deep breath, finally answering, "I'm not really sure, Lieutenant. She wore a scarf over her head, tied under her chin."

"How could you determine her age, then?"

He smiled primly. "She was wearing slacks. And I could see that she was—broader in the beam than a young woman."

"How long did they talk?"

"Just a minute. Maybe less. They might've just said a word or two to each other. Then the woman went on walking."

"She could have been a stranger to the girl, then."

He raised his narrow shoulders. "I really couldn't say."

"What happened next, Mr. Farley?"

"Well, next—" As he paused, I saw his pale eyes quicken, lit by some strange, secret memory. "Next she walked up the slope to where they—they found her."

"Was she alone?"

He nodded.

"Were the man and the boy in the area?"

"I—I didn't see them."

"What about the woman? Was she there?"

"No, she'd gone. Almost everyone had gone. Even the popcorn man was getting ready to go. His truck was all closed up, I remember. It was getting dark and cold."

"If almost everyone else had gone, Mr. Farley, then that leaves you. Have you thought about that? You were almost the last one to see her alive. You, and the murderer."

His tongue-tip circled his lips. His wide, innocent eyes didn't falter. He nodded slowly. "Yes," he whispered. "That's what Mother said, too."

I lowered my voice to match his, saying, "Did your mother tell you to come down here, Mr. Farley?"

"Yes. When I remembered it all, she said I should come down."

I allowed a long moment of silence to pass before I leaned toward him, almost intimately. "What did you do," I asked softly, "when you saw June Towers going up the slope?"

"I went on toward Fulton," he answered promptly. "I was late for dinner, you see. And it was getting dark."

I rose to my feet, glancing a last time at my watch. "I'm afraid I've got to be going, Mr. Farley. But I want to thank you very much for volunteering this information." I paused, then asked, "By the way, do you remember seeing a dark-haired, middle-aged man sitting in a white Ford?"

He began to shake his head, then caught himself. "As a matter of fact," he said slowly, "I think I do." He thought about it, frowning, nibbling at his lip. Then, decisively, he bobbed his head. "Yes. I *do* remember a man in a white Ford. He was parked across from the popcorn wagon, on the opposite side of the street. He was just sitting there, though. He didn't get out of his car."

I thanked him and promised to contact him tomorrow. The thought seemed to please him, and he left my office smiling.

As he closed the door my phone rang.

"Lieutenant Hastings," I said.

"I have a phone call for you, Lieutenant." It was Manley in Communications. "It sounds—" He hesitated. "It sounds heavy. I know you're interrogating, but I thought I ought to take a chance with this one."

Manley wore his hair borderline-long, and some considered his handlebar mustache subversive. But he had a good ear and he wasn't afraid to think for himself.

"All right, let's have it. Then see if you can find Inspector Canelli for me, will you?"

"Yessir."

112

The line clicked. Then I heard someone breathing unevenly. "This is Lieutenant Hastings," I said.

The breathing continued. There was no noise in the background—nothing identifiable.

"Who's this?" I asked.

"It—" The caller cleared his throat. "It's Kent, Lieutenant. Kent Miller."

"What can I do for you, Kent?"

"Well, I—" Again he cleared his throat. "I've been thinking. And I—I guess I better talk to you."

"Where are you?"

"I'm—at home."

"All right. We'll be there in fifteen or twenty minutes. Three-fifteen, say."

"Okay, Lieutenant. Thanks."

Nineteen

I rang the Millers' bell a third time.

"I can hear the bell," Canelli offered. "Plain as day."

I tried the door. The knob turned; the door swung open. I stepped into the quiet hallway.

"Kent?"

Behind me, I could hear Canelli sniffing. "Oh, oh," he whispered.

The odor was unmistakable: the excremental, blood-clotting stench of sudden death.

Drawing my revolver, I whispered, "You cover the back."

I closed the front door behind me, using my heel. The latch-click was loud in the uneasy silence of the house. I stood perfectly still, listening. Nothing stirred.

Just ahead was the open archway leading into the living room. Very slowly, gun held ready, I stepped forward.

He lay face down, his torso on the couch, his thighs across a marble coffee table. He was dressed as I'd seen him earlier, in suntan trousers and a Levi jacket. His head was jammed against the couch-back at a cruel, neck-broken angle. The table had collapsed under the impact. His legs and arms were flung

114

wide, spread-eagled. The blood-mess at the back of his tangled blond head was still a bright, oozing red.

Only minutes before he'd been alive.

Was the murderer running? Hiding?

Could the murderer hear me—see me?

Pivoting slowly away from the body, I cocked my gun. The two hammer-clicks were the only sounds in the stillness. Tiptoeing, I glanced behind the sofa, then scanned the room for another hiding place. A narrow door flanked the ornate Spanish-style fireplace. With my back to the wall, I slowly rotated the doorknob. It turned freely.

Crouching, I flung the door wide.

Fireplace logs were stacked neatly inside.

I moved into the hallway. The dining room was crowded with gleaming, store-new mahogany furniture and a sparkling display of sideboard crystal. There was no closet—no place to hide. I stepped to the hallway window, offering a narrow view of the garden.

Nothing stirred.

Reentering the hallway, again I stood motionless, listening. From outside, I could hear the faint sound of laughing children. A motorcycle was passing. A truck rumbled by slowly.

Ahead, on my left, three doors were closed. Walking softly, I carefully checked each door-crack. If he was hiding in one of the three rooms, and came out shooting, a latch-click could be our only warning.

The kitchen was ahead, with only one inside door, doubtless leading to the basement.

Picking a crumpled paper napkin from the food-cluttered table, I carefully opened the back door, gripping only the knob-stem.

Canelli stood on the narrow back porch. He held his gun down along his leg, concealed from casual scrutiny.

Forefinger to my lips, I motioned him inside. Using hand signals, we searched the two bedrooms and the bath. The basement-garage yielded nothing. There was no attic. We found nothing disturbed—no indication of forced entry or robbery.

Yet the boy's blood was still wet. He hadn't been dead more than twenty minutes.

Handling the phone carefully, I called Manley in Communications.

"Is Lieutenant Friedman in?" I asked.

"No, sir. He's—just a moment, please." I heard a flip of pages. "He's on his way to the Grant residence. Do you want me to get him for you?"

"No. I want you to give him a message. Tell him that Kent Miller has just been killed. Murdered. The address is 2417 Balboa. Ask Lieutenant Friedman to come here as soon as he can. Clear?"

"Yessir."

"All right. Is Insp—Sergeant Markham in?"

"No. He's with Lieutenant Friedman."

"Give me Culligan, then."

"Yessir."

A moment later Culligan's dry, slightly nasal voice came on the line. Whatever he said, Culligan seemed to be complaining.

"Have you got a pencil?" I asked.

"Yes."

"Kent Miller has just been murdered. It had to've happened between three-ten and three-thirty. That's important—the time. It's now three forty-two."

"Right."

"How many men have we got available?"

"Four. Including me."

"Well, I want you to stay inside, with the phone. Lieutenant Friedman is coming over here, to the scene. So you're the only one catching. Clear?"

"Yes."

"Okay. Here's what I want you to do: send teams—they'll have to be an inspector and a uniformed man, I guess—to interrogate Lester Farley, the Fishers, and Walter Cross. I want to know where each one of them was between three and three-thirty."

"All the Fishers, you mean?"

"Yes. But especially James. Naturally."

"All right. Anything else?"

"No. But I want you to really move. It's possible that the murderer is on his way home. You understand?"

"Yes."

"Give me Manley again, then."

Manley's voice was tight as he asked me to hold. Then: "I've just got Lieutenant Friedman on the phone, Lieutenant. Just this second."

"Good. Let me talk to him."

"What is it?" Friedman asked. From the sound of his voice, I knew that he was phoning from the Grant house.

"Kent Miller's dead. Murdered less than a half-hour ago, probably. Can you come over?"

"What's the address?"

"2417 Balboa. It's two and a half blocks from you."

"No problem."

"Is Grant there?"

"No."

In the momentary silence that followed, we both shared the other's thoughts.

"He's a little late," Friedman said dryly.

"You'd better leave Markham there."

"I was just thinking the same thing."

"We're out of personnel, downtown. Culligan's catching."

"I'll be right over."

"Good."

I told Canelli to call the technicians, then I returned to the living room. As I walked down the hallway, I settled my revolver more comfortably on my hip, buttoning my jacket. During the next two or three minutes I would have my time alone with the corpse.

I stood between his wide-spread legs, staring down at the head.

In nine years as a policeman, I still couldn't credit the incredible rag-doll limpness of a corpse. Violent death jerks the arms, legs, and neck into grotesque, bone-bent postures, so that a body seems no more than a discarded bundle of clothing, with limbs and head protruding at odd, awkward angles.

Stepping around the smashed coffee table, involuntarily holding my breath against the odor, I stood at his right side. Eyes wide, he was staring at the sofa-arm. His nose and lips were flattened against the cushions. His teeth were tightly clenched. Between the teeth the tip of his tongue protruded, bleeding, half bitten through.

I walked in back of the sofa, standing on his left side.

His head had been badly battered. White bone-bits shone through the hair and blood; the paler pink of brain tissue mottled the darker scalp blood, now clotting. At the base of the neck, where it joined the shoulder, I saw the ragged edges of a two-inch puncture wound. A knife thrust had gone in at . . .

A doorknob rattled. I twisted toward the sound, crouching involuntarily, hand on my gun.

Friedman was moving leisurely into the archway, wrinkling his nose. "Whew. Just once I'd like to stumble across a corpse who'd voided before, not after."

"I know what you mean."

"Looks like the Towers M.O."

Turning with him toward the body, I pointed to the wound at the base of the neck. "Look at that, though."

"Stab wound," he grunted. "Where's the weapon?" He stooped for a closer look.

"Haven't found it."

"You didn't look hard enough, Lieutenant." Drawing a plastic evidence bag from his pocket, folding it between thumb and forefinger, he reached behind one of the sofa's seat cushions. "Here you are."

He was holding a pair of blood-smeared pruning shears. With blades locked together, the shears would just fit the wound.

"Shades of the potting shed," he muttered.

"What?"

"David and James Fisher use their potting shed as a clubhouse, or something. Remember? And I wouldn't be surprised to discover that these shears come from that potting shed."

He rotated the pruning shears, silently pointing to an "F" scratched in the black enameled handle. We exchanged a long look before he turned away, tucking the weapon back behind the cushions. The plastic bag was slightly blood-smeared. He eyed the smear distastefully, then carefully turned the bag inside out and gingerly returned it to his pocket.

"The Fishers are just around the corner," I said.

Twenty

I pulled up in front of the Fisher house and switched off the engine. "Think we should get reinforcements?" I asked.

"You're stalling," Friedman answered dryly. "You hate to drop a bomb on your little friend. Admit it."

"He's *not* my little friend." I'd said it more vehemently than I'd intended.

His broad face expressionless, eyes fixed on a far-distant vista, he said, "Many, many years ago I figured out that this job is exactly like wringing chickens' necks. The longer you put it off, the worse it gets."

"Let's go, then." I reached for the door handle.

"However," he continued blandly, "there's no point in not at least checking with Culligan. Circumspectly, of course." He pointed to the microphone.

Unaccountably irritated, I reached abruptly for the mike and asked for Culligan. The connection took less than fifteen seconds to complete. "I'm on the air," I said immediately. "Anything to report on the Miller 607?"

"Negative, Lieutenant."

"How many teams have reported in?"

120

"Just one. Cross. It was inconclusive."

"Have you got someone on the way to the Fisher residence?"

"Yessir."

I looked questioningly at Friedman, who first shrugged, then said, "Why don't you divert them to the Millers'? Canelli could use some help."

Nodding, I relayed the instructions, gave Culligan our destination, and signed off.

"Okay, Lieutenant," Friedman said, opening his door and laboriously swinging his chubby legs free. "Let's see who owns a pair of missing pruning shears."

Marge Fisher answered the doorbell on the first ring. In contrast to the slacks and denim apron she wore, her face was carefully made up, her hair meticulously groomed. Even doing her housework, she would keep up appearances.

"Lieutenant Hastings." As she said it, she fell back a step. Her hand was tightly clutching the apron; her eyes were fearful.

Were the frantic, furtive gestures studied or involuntary? Did her wide eyes mirror actual fear—or a quickly contrived counterfeit?

I couldn't decide.

"Is your brother-in-law in, Mrs. Fisher?"

She nodded slowly.

"Can we speak to him?"

She cleared her throat—once, twice.

Was she stalling? Giving Fisher time? Beside me, I felt Friedman moving toward the door.

"Where is he, Mrs. Fisher?" Friedman was asking.

"He—he's in back. With David."

"In the potting shed?"

She nodded.

"How long has he been there?"

"I—I don't know. I . . ." She broke off. Retreating another uncertain step, she stood with hands clasped at her waist. Her eyes moved spasmodically between the two of us. She was blinking rapidly, swallowing repeatedly. She flushed, then paled. She was going into mild shock.

"Have you been here all afternoon?" I asked.

"N—no. I—I went to the store."

"When did you leave for the store?"

"Ab—ab—" Mouth working helplessly, she could only stare at me.

"What time, Mrs. Fisher?" It was Friedman's voice, gently insistent.

Turning toward him, she said, "About two, I think."

"You left for the store at two?"

She nodded, eying Friedman with a kind of rapt, reluctant fixity.

"What time did you get back?"

"I—just a few minutes ago."

"It's four o'clock now. Have you been back for fifteen minutes?"

"I—yes. Just about."

"All right. Good." Friedman's voice had deepened to an easy, almost affable encouragement. "Now, was James home when you left?"

She nodded.

"Was he here when you arrived back home?"

"Y—yes."

"Where was he when you returned?" I asked.

She licked at her lips as she turned back to me, frowning now. "I—I don't understand."

"Was he in the potting shed?"

"I—I guess so."

"Aren't you sure, Mrs. Fisher?"

"Well, I—I'm not *really* sure. Except that every day he always waits for David there. In the potting shed. David always comes home down the alley and goes to the potting shed first before he comes into the house. So I—" She shrugged helplessly.

"What time does David get home from school?"

"About three-thirty."

"Is he in the potting shed now? Are they together?"

"I—I— Yes, I guess so. Is—is something wrong?" As she said it she twisted suddenly to look back over her shoulder.

Friedman stepped forward. "There's nothing wrong, Mrs. Fisher. But we have to talk to James. How do we get to the potting shed?"

Unclasping her hands, she pointed back through the house. "You can go through the kitchen."

We walked quickly through the house. Standing on the back porch, we paused, looking at the small shingled shed.

Like everything the Fishers owned, the potting shed was immaculately conceived: an outsized playhouse, studied, contrived. From inside the shed, through the small, picturesque window, I caught a flicker of movement.

"He's in there," I said softly.

"Someone's in there, anyhow. I wish to hell we had those shears."

"We can get them later."

"Ready?"

"Yes."

Pacing slowly side by side, we walked across the golf-green grass, ignoring the neat flagstone pathway. As we walked I glanced up at the sky. Dark clouds were gathering in the west. During the night it would surely rain.

"The first thing," Friedman said, "let's get rid of the kid. Send him into the house so he won't pick up any cues from Uncle James."

"Right."

"You go first."

I moved ahead, turning the shingled corner. The clapboard door, with its ostentatiously old-fashioned hardware, faced a six-foot cyclone fence separating the Fishers' lot from the alleyway. The alley, I knew, led directly to the back of the Miller house, a block and a half away. The alleyway gate was directly in back of the potting shed, concealed from the Fisher house.

"This is a setup," Friedman whispered. "From the house, no

one could see him leave. He could've gotten into the alley, over to the Millers' and back—all in a few minutes. No one inside the house would be the wiser, providing they didn't come out into the backyard."

Nodding, unbuttoning my jacket, I knocked on the picture-book door. Friedman stood to one side, listening intently. As the latch clicked, I tensed, crouching, ready.

The boy stood in the open doorway, looking up at me with his refugee's eyes. The uncle stood behind the boy, motionless. I was again struck by the similarity of the two faces: pale, narrow, and sad, with somber dark eyes and wide, vulnerable mouths.

I looked down at the boy. "Your mother would like to see you in the house, David."

"B—but—"

I stepped aside, making room for him to pass. "Hurry up, David. She's waiting."

Moving one single, reluctant step at a time, he edged past me, only to stop, turn back, and stand looking up at his uncle. Slowly the man nodded to the boy, moving his head toward the house. The man's mouth stirred in a slight, wistful smile. Finally the boy turned silently away.

It was yesterday's tableau, repeated.

I let Friedman go inside, then closed the door behind us. Like the house and the boy's room, the potting shed was immaculate, compulsively ordered. Clay pots were stacked by size and shape. Several large plastic bins were filled with dirt, sand, leaf mold, and peat moss, all neatly labeled. Half of one wall was covered by a pegboard tool rack. The pegboard was painted a light green. Each tool was meticulously outlined in red.

A handsaw was missing.

And a small pair of pruning shears.

Catching Friedman's eye, I moved my head toward the tool rack. Almost imperceptibly, he nodded. Together we turned toward James Fisher.

He stood with his back to a low bench, hands braced wide to

124

either side, fingers resting on the bench. Yet his posture wasn't fearful or rigid. He seemed relaxed, at ease. His expression was almost quizzical.

I pointed to the rack. "Do you mind telling me where I could find that pair of pruning shears, Mr. Fisher? The pair that's missing."

He looked puzzled. "I can't tell you, Lieutenant. All day they've been missing. I've looked for them."

"Would you describe the shears for us?" Friedman asked.

"They're about twelve inches long," Fisher answered readily, "with a black handle. Why? Did you find them?" His dark, pensive eyes were guileless as he turned toward Friedman.

"We may have," Friedman said. "When did they turn up missing?"

"Today," Fisher replied. "Just today."

"In the afternoon or the morning?"

"About lunchtime, I'd say. I came here after lunch. I was going to trim the junipers. And I—I couldn't find the shears."

"Did the shears have the letter 'F' scratched on the handle?"

"Yes, they did."

I allowed a moment of silence to pass as we both watched the suspect's reaction, expecting him to query us further concerning our knowledge of the shears.

"What about the saw?" I finally asked. "What happened to that?"

Fisher's inscrutable gaze moved hesitantly to meet mine. "It's being sharpened." Now he was vaguely troubled. "It's been gone for two days, at least."

"So only the pruning shears are unaccounted for. We know what happened to the saw. Is that right?"

Slowly he nodded.

"Is the potting shed kept locked?"

Again he nodded—still meeting my eyes, unblinking.

"Is it locked during the day? Or just at night?"

"It's locked all the time."

"Who has a key, besides yourself?"

His lips moved in a wry, regretful smile. "I don't have a key, Lieutenant. Only my brother and sister-in-law have keys."

"How do you get into the shed, then?"

"David and I use the so-called 'secret key.' It's kept on a nail hammered into the plum tree. David and I share it."

"Have you been at home all day?" Friedman asked.

"Yes. All day."

"Out here, most of the time? In the potting shed?"

"Since lunch, yes."

"During the time you were out here, did you see anyone?" Fisher frowned, perplexed. "I—I don't understand."

"I want to know," Friedman said, "whether you saw anyone from, say, two o'clock until now. Did you speak to anyone? Did anyone speak to you?"

"Just David. He—" Fisher hesitated. His eyes were clouding; he was staring at Friedman with sad disbelief. His voice dropped to a low, deadened monotone as he said, "It's happening again, isn't it?"

Exchanging a glance with Friedman, I said quietly, "We've got to have an account of your movements from two o'clock until now, Mr. Fisher. Your sister-in-law can't help us. Neither can David, apparently. Is there anyone else?"

He shook his head regretfully. "I told you yesterday, Lieutenant: time isn't the same for me as it is for—for other people. I—I can't keep track of it. Time is my enemy."

"Time is everyone's enemy," Friedman muttered.

Nodding in tentative, timid overture, Fisher said, "You know, then. You know about time."

Friedman said dryly, "Everyone over forty knows, Mr. Fisher. It's no secret."

"You're good men," Fisher said softly. "You're not like the others—the ones before. You're good men. You—you understand what you're doing. You understand what it means—how you make people feel." He spoke as if he were pronouncing a benediction. His eyes were soft, regretful.

Friedman's expression was impassive.

"But you've come to arrest me," Fisher said finally. "You're

126

going to take me to a small room. And then you'll lock me up. First you'll question me. Then you'll lock me up."

I heard Friedman sigh deeply. But his eyes were still impassively steady as he said, "Yes, Mr. Fisher. We've got to take you downtown with us. We've got to question you, at least. And we've got to conduct some examinations. But before we do, we want you to know that you have the right to remain silent. You have the right to . . ."

"I know," Fisher interrupted gently. "Lieutenant Hastings told me that yesterday."

"Were you wearing those clothes all day?" I asked.

Fisher dropped his eyes, looking down at his clothing. He nodded. Then he asked, "Can we go out through the alleyway, Lieutenant? If we go out through the front, the children will see us. And they'll tease David. They'll . . ."

Behind me, the door came open. David stood in the doorway. His mother was behind him. Plainly, she'd tried to restrain him, unsuccessfully. I heard Friedman mutter something, swearing under his breath.

Momentarily no one spoke. Then, standing with legs braced wide, fists clenched at his sides, the boy said, "I hate you. Both of you. You're both just—just bullies." His voice was high, cracked. His eyes were very bright. His chin was trembling. Behind him, the mother was plucking at the boy. Her hands were fretful on his shoulder.

I heard the uncle whisper, "They're not bullies, David. They —they just want to talk to me. It'll be all right. I promise you."

"I didn't lie about Sunday. They say I did. But I didn't. I *didn't.*"

"It's not about Sunday, David. It's about today. Something happened today. And they want to talk to me about it. That's all."

"What happened today? What was it?"

Exchanging a glance with Friedman, I realized that I was thankful for his presence—and for his senior rank. The responsibility for the next minutes was his.

Moving with heavy deliberation, Friedman beckoned the

woman and the boy inside and pulled the door closed. I watched David run to his uncle's side. On the workbench, the man's long, quiet fingers covered the boy's hand. David looked up into his uncle's face, then quickly away, swallowing painfully. Standing apart, the mother watched the boy with bright, baleful eyes.

"About an hour ago," Friedman said, "a teen-ager named Kent Miller was murdered, just a block and a half from here. He was June Towers' boyfriend, so we're almost certain the two murders are connected. A pair of pruning shears were found beside the body." He pointed to the green pegboard. "The description of those shears matches the description of yours. And nobody here can tell me why those shears are missing." He turned to face Marge Fisher. "Can you tell me, Mrs. Fisher?"

"N—no."

"Can you, David?"

The boy was mutely shaking his head. His eyes seemed unfocused. He was obviously thinking feverishly.

"Then you all know as much as we do." Friedman's voice was brisk, businesslike. Addressing the woman, he said, "We've already explained Mr. Fisher's constitutional rights to him. I'm sure you'll want to contact your husband and arrange for a lawyer. In the meantime, we've got no alternative but to take Mr. Fisher downtown for questioning. Partly, it's for his own good. We'll examine his clothes for, ah, physical evidence, and we'll examine the pruning shears. When we've done that, we'll all know better where we stand. One thing is for sure, though: without conducting these examinations, we can't clear him. Not now. So, in a way, it's better for all concerned that . . ."

"I saw the man in the white car," the boy was saying softly. "Just this morning, I saw him. In the alley."

With his eyes, wearily, Friedman indicated that it was my turn.

"What time this morning, David?" My voice, I knew, was toneless. I found myself avoiding his dark, anxious eyes.

128

Hiding Place

"I was just going to school. I always go out the back gate—out through the alley. But then—" He paused in his headlong word-rush. "But then, just after I got around the corner, I remembered that I'd left my notebook in the potting shed, from the night before. So I—I had to come back and get it. And so I—" Glancing from me to Friedman, transparently calculating the effect of his story, he licked at his lips. "I came back to get the book. And that's when I saw him."

"Was he in the same white car?"

"No. He was walking. But he was the same man. I—I recognized him right off. I—I think I've even seen him around here before. Even before I saw him in the park. I *know* I did."

"How did you recognize him?" I asked quietly.

He swallowed. "How?"

"Yes. Was he wearing the same clothes?"

Watching me warily, he said cautiously, "I—I think so."

"What was he wearing today?" I asked.

"A—a jacket. A brown jacket."

"What kind of pants?"

"They were brown, too. A darker brown."

"And he was wearing the same jacket when you saw him Sunday, in the park. Is that right?"

"Yes. It was the same. Exactly the same."

"How about the pants? Were they the same, too?"

He nodded.

For a long, silent moment I stood looking down at him. Then, almost regretfully, I asked, "Did the man get out of the car on Sunday, David?"

He began to shake his head, then quickly arrested the movement. Now he stood rigidly, small fists clenched at his sides. He'd discovered the trap.

"He didn't get out of the car on Sunday, did he, David?"

His lower lip was trembling. "I saw him," he whispered fiercely. "And you can't make me say I didn't. I saw him both days. And this morning I know what he did. I *know* it. He—he watched me get my books from the shed. He saw me get the key. And then he went in and stole the shears. I—I *know* that's what happened."

"How do you know it, David?"

"Because th—that's the only way it could've happened. When I got my—my books, the shears were there. I—I *saw* them."

I turned toward the pegboard, silently compelling him to turn with me. I could sense my own laggard reluctance as I said, "How about the saw, David? Was that there, too?"

Licking his lips, he was staring at the empty space. Finally: "Yes. That was there, too."

I looked from the boy to the man. Head bowed, James Fisher was shaking his head slowly, hopelessly.

I finished the job: "They were both there this morning, then —both the saw and the shears. You're sure of it."

The boy nodded desperately. His eyes were locked with mine pleadingly. I looked away, toward Friedman. In response, Friedman stepped forward. His beefy arms were half raised, herding the boy and the mother outside.

"We've got to be going," Friedman was saying. "We've got a homicide that's not much more than an hour old."

Marge Fisher took the boy's elbow, turning him toward the door. "Come on, David. We can . . ."

Suddenly whirling wildly away, the boy hurled himself at the door. The impact sprung the latch; the door swung open. Off balance, the boy stumbled to his knees in the doorway. Scrabbling, he turned in the dirt to face us, at bay. As his mother reached down for him, he fiercely pulled away, sobbing. Eyes wild, he screamed up at her, "You did it. I *know* you did. It—it's all your fault. I know it's all your fault. You've hated James, always. And you won't help him. You're going to let them lock him up, just like you did before. And this time he—he'll die. They'll kill him, this time. They'll . . ."

"*David. Don't.* You can't. You—" Sobbing, she fell awkwardly to her knees beside him, reaching out. The boy leaped to his feet, twisted away and disappeared. I could hear the fad-

130

ing sound of his sobbing. Then I heard the back door slam violently.

Still on her knees, the woman turned toward James Fisher. Her face was a streaked, ruined mask of malevolence. Her lips were drawn back, revealing tight-clenched teeth. "Are you satisfied now?" she whispered. "Now are you satisfied? You—you animal."

She staggered to her feet. I could hear her sobs, too, crossing the yard toward the house.

Twenty-one

I waited for Friedman and Fisher to step out into the hallway, then I closed and locked the door of the tiny cagelike prisoner's elevator.

Friedman drew me aside, gesturing for Fisher to sit on a long wooden bench. "Why don't you interrogate him?" Friedman said softly. "I'll see what's been happening in the field. Shall I send Culligan in to you?"

"I won't need him."

"Where'll you be?"

"In my office."

Friedman's quick, shrewd glance was speculative. Regulations stated that all bona-fide suspects must be questioned in locked interrogation rooms, with two officers inside and one officer posted in the corridor.

"Don't worry," I said. "He's not violent."

"I once spent a month in the hospital after interrogating a nonviolent suspect."

I shrugged. For a moment we eyed each other, engaged in a minor contest of wills. Finally Friedman lifted his beefy shoulders in a shrug of grudging acquiescence.

"I'll prepare the booking papers," he said. "Provided, of course, that David hasn't confessed to both murders."

Exchanging another long look, we mutely agreed that it hadn't been a very good joke. I turned away, brusquely signaling the prisoner to his feet.

"Sit down, Mr. Fisher." I gestured to my visitor's armchair.

He looked down at the chair. After examining it, he turned deliberately, flexed his knees, and slowly lowered himself into the chair. He moved as if each motion required a separate act of will.

"Do you understand why you're here?" I asked finally.

"Yes, I understand." His voice was totally uninflected: a hollow-sounding automaton's voice, matching his mechanical movements.

"In a little while," I said, "we're going to bring you some other clothes."

He nodded somberly. "Jail clothes."

"No, Mr. Fisher. They're not jail clothes. In fact, if you like, I'll ask your relatives to bring you some of your own clothes."

He sat with his hands folded in his lap, one hand covering the other, looking down at them pensively. At intervals he moved the topmost hand, slowly stroking the one beneath.

"We need the clothes you're wearing for the laboratory—for analysis. When the technicians are finished—if the results are negative—you'll get the clothes back."

Head still bowed, he said, so low I could barely hear him, "Negative, that means I'm safe. But positive means murder."

I sighed. "Do you want some clothes from your home, Mr. Fisher?"

"No." He sat quietly, head lowered as though in prayer. He was leaning slightly forward. His knees and feet were together. His shoulders were rounded. It was an ascetic, monastic posture. "It's not my home," he said tonelessly. "So my clothes can't be there if I'm not. Because everything I have is where I am. You live inside your clothes. Deep down inside your clothes, hiding." He paused. Then: "But you won't find any blood."

"Then you'll be in good shape," I answered.

Again his lips stirred, smiling slightly. "Yes, I'll be in good shape."

We sat quietly, neither of us moving. Finally: "I'll be back in a small room," he said. "It's where it all started: in a small room. And that's where it should end. Because, you see, that's where I'm safest. I'm locked in, and they're locked out. I tried to tell them that in Graceville. I tried to tell them that I should stay— that I *wanted* to stay. But then they told me that I was cured and I had to go home. But what they really meant, you see, was that they wanted my room for someone else. So they asked Bill to take me home. That's what they called it, home. But they shouldn't. Because words are just words, and love isn't always the right word. Not really. Not always. Not when you grow up and feel the world slipping away from you. Because, then, you've got to hold on with both hands. And that's all you have— just two hands. So, really, you're helpless. Even if you want to, and it's all slipping away, you can't touch anyone, because you only have two hands. Th—that's what happened to me, you know. And to David, too—that's what's happening to him."

"Did David lie, Mr. Fisher? Did he lie, to protect you?"

"Yes, he lied. You could've seen it in his eyes if you'd really looked."

I sat for a moment, debating whether to go on with it. Finally I decided to wait for the lab reports. I summoned Culligan to my office, scribbling a note that instructed him to get the lab tests started, meanwhile confining James Fisher in a private holding cell, pending the results of the tests.

As Culligan waited for Fisher to rise from the visitor's chair, my phone rang. With a feeling of relief at the interruption, I picked up the receiver.

"Lieutenant Hastings."

"It's Ann, Frank."

"Hi."

"Are you busy?"

The prisoner walked slowly out into the hallway, still with his hands clasped, head bowed, shoulders hunched forward.

"No," I answered, watching the door close. "No, I'm not busy. Not now."

"I just wanted to tell you that Thursday isn't good for dinner, after all. Billy's having a play rehearsal. Can you come tomorrow night?"

"I think so. Unless something new comes up."

She hesitated. Glancing at my watch, I was surprised to discover that it was five o'clock. She would be phoning from home.

"Does that mean that your—your current case is finished?" she asked.

"I think so. That's the way it looks."

"Is my—my friend involved?"

"I'm afraid so. Indirectly."

I heard her sigh. "I'm sorry, darling," she said slowly. "I really am sorry. For you, I mean."

"Ann, you . . ."

"And I'm sorry for having said it," she interrupted quickly. "I've been thinking about our—our conversation the other night. And I can see that it doesn't help you, for me to talk about it. Even telling you that I'm trying to understand doesn't help, because I *can't* understand. There's no way. And I—I see that now. But I just had to know about David."

"I know. I'll tell you about it later."

"All right. I'll let you go now, darling. I won't say any more about it. I promise. I'll see you tomorrow."

"About six?"

"Yes."

"I'll bring a bottle of wine."

"All right. Goodbye, Frank."

I replaced the receiver in its cradle, then just sat there idly touching the buttons at the base of the phone, lightly brushing the clear plastic cubes with the tips of my fingers.

The phone with its five plastic buttons was a status symbol. I had a private office, and a clothes rack, and a walnut desk, and a phone with five buttons. I'd been to college. I'd played injury-ridden second-string professional football, badly. I'd married an heiress, and fathered two good-looking, incredibly poised children. I'd worked for my father-in-law, entertaining too many important clients with too many drinks at too many bars. I'd . . .

A knock sounded, I recognized the characteristic tattoo. It was Friedman.

"Come in." I swiveled to face the door.

Carrying a manila folder, Friedman sank heavily into the armchair and haphazardly tossed the folder on my desk. "How'd it go?" he asked, taking a cigar from an inside pocket.

"He admitted that the boy lied. If the clothes check out positive, we've got a case that we can take to the D.A."

"Did the boy lie both times—about both days?"

"He didn't say."

"Didn't you ask?"

"No."

Grunting noncommittally, he rummaged unsuccessfully for a match. I opened my center desk drawer and threw a book of matches across the desk.

"Maybe it's all coming together," Friedman said, tossing his still-smoking match into my wastebasket.

I banged my drawer closed and pushed an ashtray across the desk, at the same time staring pointedly at my wastebasket. If a fire ever started, it would . . .

"Where's Fisher now?" Friedman asked.

"Culligan's got him—getting his clothes for the lab. Have you filled out the papers?"

"Yes."

"What's in there?" I pointed to the manila folder. "The field reports from today?"

He nodded, snorting ruefully. "It's all just a big bunch of nothing, really. Christ, I never realized it until today, when I actually got out there, but all the victims and all the suspects are living in each other's back pockets. And then, when you figure in those alleys—" He shrugged. "They might as well be connected to each other by secret passageways."

"Were they all accounted for between three and three-thirty?"

"They were *none* of them accounted for. Not really." He lifted his eyes to the ceiling, organizing his thoughts. Then, recit-

136

ing elaborately, he intoned: "Walter Cross said he was home, drinking. Which, according to the examining officer, he very well could've been, since he was pretty well potted. Lester Farley was out—and is still out. Randall Grant got home at approximately three forty-five. He said he stopped off for a drink—and he had alcoholic breath. I left Ellen Grant's at approximately quarter to three, and didn't return until I talked to you, which Manley tells me was 3:27 P.M. So Ellen could've gone out and come back without my knowing. She said she was home, though—but she didn't have any witnesses."

"What about Bill Fisher? Did anyone check him?"

Surprised, Friedman raised his eyebrows. After pausing to blow a leisurely smoke ring, he said, "Is Bill Fisher a suspect? I didn't know."

"I was just curious. The wife was out. I just wondered about the husband."

"What do you propose for a motive, where the Fishers are concerned?"

"Oh, come on, Pete—" I shifted irritably in my chair. "Let's—" I broke off. To my surprise, I was angry. "Let's get on with it, instead of teasing it to death."

For a moment, puffing on the cigar, he didn't respond. Irritably, I flopped out my hand, deliberately knuckle-rapping the desk. "I'm sorry," I muttered. "I—I've about had it with this case. If we've got it wrapped up, let's wrap it up—and go home."

Leaning forward, he deposited a long ash in my ashtray. "The next move is up to the lab," he said, as if I didn't know the whole procedure. "And then the D.A. Pretty soon we'll be off the hook. We're meeting tomorrow at one o'clock with the D.A. guy. By that time we'll have a lab report on the pruning shears and Fisher's clothing. Marge Fisher and the boy both identified the shears, incidentally. Markham took the shears by their house." He paused. I could feel his eyes on me, but I didn't look up. Suddenly his voice irritated me. "Why don't you go home?" he said. "Go through the garage if you want to give the reporters the slip. I'll stay here for a few minutes—to keep my eye on your wastebasket for you. Just in case."

About to retort sharply, I suddenly realized that I was smiling. Without a word I rose to my feet, got my hat, and left the office.

"Don't forget," he called after me, "we've got a date at one o'clock."

The door had already swung shut behind me.

Twenty-two

"Well," Friedman said heavily, sailing the lab report across the conference table to Mel Segal from the D.A.'s office. "The lab boys and the coroner really weren't very helpful. They told us what we already knew: that the shears inflicted the neck wound, but that the traditional round, blunt instrument did the actual damage. Also, they couldn't find any trace of blood on either the suspect's clothing or his hands. And so far, no one's been able to locate the round blunt instrument."

"Are you sure the suspect couldn't have changed his clothes?" Segal asked, adjusting a pair of heavy horned-rimmed reading glasses.

"He *could* have, but he didn't. At least two neighbors have said that he wore the same . . ."

Behind me, the conference room phone buzzed discreetly. Murmuring an apology, I picked up the phone. "Lieutenant Hastings," I said softly.

"It's Canelli, Lieutenant. Say, I know I shouldn't be bothering you right now. And I been thinking about it for five or ten minutes, at least. We've notified the black-and-white cars, and everything. But I thought you ought to know."

139

"Ought to know what, Canelli?" I asked wearily.

"That David Fisher's come up missing. He was supposed to come home from school for lunch, and he didn't show. So his mother checked, and he never made it to school. So naturally, she's all upset. And like I say, it's on the air, and I made sure that Manley gave it a little extra heat. But I thought that—"

"Where are you?"

"At my desk."

"Get the car. I'll meet you out in front."

As we pulled up in front of the Fisher house, I saw Bill Fisher just entering his own front door. Canelli set the parking brake and I cleared our car with Communications.

As we walked to the door Canelli was saying, "You don't suppose the kid was telling the truth all the time, do you?"

"No, I don't."

"What about yesterday morning, though? What if he really did see the dark guy who'd been in the park? I mean, with the lab tests negative and everything, it's beginning to look like a different ball game." He hesitated. "Isn't it?"

I sighed. "When I figure it out, Canelli, I promise you'll be the first to know." I pressed the Fishers' bell, avoiding Canelli's moist, reproachful stare.

The door came quickly open. Today Marge Fisher's hair was disarranged, her make-up hastily and haphazardly applied. She wore denim slacks and a brightly flowered blouse.

"Have you found him?" she demanded. She stood squarely before us, as if to bar our entrance.

"Not yet, Mrs. Fisher. Have you heard anything?"

She shook her head sharply. Her eyes were very bright. Her mouth twitched. "No. Nothing."

I nodded toward the inside hallway. "May we come in?"

"Oh. Yes." She stepped aside grudgingly. Bill Fisher, wearing slacks and a khaki jacket, was seated in the same chair he'd occupied Monday evening when we'd first come to the house.

Gripping the chair-arms, Fisher half rose. "Did you get him?"

"No. But we will."

Hiding Place

As Canelli and I sat on the couch, the woman perched uncomfortably on a straight-backed chair. Immediately she clasped her hands tightly in her lap. Her painfully corded throat moved convulsively as she swallowed repeatedly. Her eyes moved constantly around the room, distractedly—as if she were looking for escape.

"But where could he have gone?" Fisher was saying. "Where *is* he, anyway?"

"Have you got a guess?" I asked.

His harried glance seemed almost furtive as he looked at me, then quickly away. His big-knuckled fist softly banged the arm of the chair, absently beating out a frustrated, furious rhythm. "If that kid's run off," he said dully, "I swear to God I'll—I'll—" Mouth working impotently, he couldn't finish it.

"Do you think he ran away?"

Bill Fisher's only answer was a sharp, savage head-shake. "I don't know." His words and gestures were angry, but his eyes looked frightened. His manliness couldn't sustain a show of fear—only anger.

"What about you, Mrs. Fisher?" I asked, turning to face her. "Do you think he ran away?"

"I don't know either," she mumbled, avoiding looking at me. "I—I just don't understand it." She glanced toward her husband. Fisher was still tapping impotently at the arm of the chair.

"Do you mind if we look in David's room?"

Both shrugged in desultory unison, not looking at each other. Responding to my nod, Canelli got to his feet and headed for the hallway.

Dropping my voice to a more authoritative note, I said, "You're both going to have to cooperate with me, you know, if we're going to find David."

The woman licked her lips. Obviously exerting a desperate effort of will, she finally met my eyes. "Wh—what d'you want to know?" Her voice was dull, her eyes dead.

"I want to know, for a start, what you think happened to David. Was he unhappy about his uncle's being in custody—abnormally unhappy? Did he threaten to run away?"

141

She shook her head doggedly. "No," she said in a low, defeated voice. "No, he didn't threaten to run away."

"Was he unhappy—terribly unhappy?"

She nodded silently. Plainly, she was exhausted, drained. She sat slack in the narrow chair—shoulders hunched, legs slung out at odd, apathetic angles. Her hands now lay listless in her lap.

"Was he . . ."

"He blames it all on us," Fisher suddenly blurted. "Everything —the whole goddamn thing. Last night he was hysterical. She won't admit it, but he was. He locked himself in his room and he was carrying on like some—some raving maniac, or something. He was like a—a wild child. I finally had to break the door in. And when I got inside, he—he backed away from me, screaming, until finally he was all jammed into a corner, like he—he was some kind of an animal in a cage, or something. It—" He drew a deep, unsteady breath. His eyes were tear-glazed. "It was terrible," he finally finished. "Just terrible. He even said that he—he wished he was dead. He—he said he wanted to die."

I allowed a moment of silence to pass before asking, "When did this happen? At what time last night?"

"Ab—about seven-thirty, I guess." Fisher paused, furtively wiping his eyes. "At least, that's when it started. After dinner."

"How'd it finally end?"

"Well, he—he just wanted us to leave him alone. And after I broke in, and saw him just—just cowering there, I—we—decided that's what we should do: leave him alone. So—" Shaking his head, he helplessly shrugged. "So that's what we did. Eventually he went to sleep. It must've been midnight."

I turned to the woman. She sat as before, inert, gazing down at the carpet. Her eyes were empty. She seemed neither grief-racked nor frightened, but instead, almost catatonic—nervelessly waiting, without hope.

"Do you have anything to add, Mrs. Fisher?"

"No," she whispered. "Nothing."

"Are you sure?"

With obvious effort she raised her head, blankly responding

142

to the edge I'd put on my voice. Then, almost indifferently, she let her neck go slack. "I'm sure."

"Did you hear David say that he wanted to die?"

She nodded.

"Did you interpret that as a possible threat of suicide?"

She made no response. She seemed to be sunk deep within herself. I sat watching her. She didn't stir. Finally, in a deliberately demanding voice, I asked, "What happened this morning? How did David seem?"

She roused herself. "He was quiet. He wouldn't talk. But he seemed all right."

"Did he say he was going to school?"

"I—I think so. At least, he didn't say he *wasn't* going."

"What was he wearing?"

"Blue jeans and a yellow rain jacket."

"Was he carrying anything?"

"No."

"Was he riding a bike?"

"Yes."

"What type of bike is it?"

She could only shrug.

"It's a lightweight," Fisher said. "Five speed. Red. It's . . ."

The phone rang. I got to my feet. "That could be for me." I walked past them into the hallway, answering the phone on its second ring.

"This is Manley, Lieutenant."

"Yes. Anything?"

"Unit Charlie Eighteen just called in to say that a boy wearing a yellow jacket was seen in the vicinity of Balboa and Twenty-seventh Avenue."

"How long ago was he seen?" As I asked the question I turned toward the living room, moving with the phone so that I could see the parents' reaction. Bill Fisher rose slowly to his feet, facing me. His wife still sat in the chair, unmoving. It was as if she hadn't heard me speaking.

"Six, seven minutes ago. Approximately one-forty P.M.," Manley answered.

143

"Can you hook me up to Charlie Eighteen?"

"Yessir. They're standing by. Just a second."

A moment later a crackle-blurred voice said, "Charlie Eighteen, sir. Jim O'Brien."

I turned away from the Fishers, facing the wall. "Hello, O'Brien. What've you got?"

"We were proceeding east on Balboa. We hadn't heard the first Fisher call; we'd been cleared, investigating a possible 302 at Thirty-seventh Avenue and Cabrillo. We saw a male Caucasian boy, age ten or eleven, wearing blue jeans and a yellow jacket."

"What kind of a jacket?"

"Lightweight plastic—one of those shells, I think you call them."

"What color was his hair?"

"Reddish."

"All right. Go ahead."

"The subject was proceeding west on Balboa, walking on the south side of the—"

"Walking?"

"Yessir."

"He wasn't wheeling a bike?"

"No, sir."

"All right. What happened?"

"Well, I looked him over, because—well, because he was acting a little odd. I had the impression that he might be in trouble —that he wanted us to stop. And we were just pulling over when we got a Code Two call at California Street and Twenty-first Avenue—an attempted 531 in progress. That's where we are now. So when I heard the Fisher supplemental, I called in."

"As soon as you're released—I'll get you released—I want you to go back to where you saw him. Hook into Tach Three. I'll be in my car. Manley, are you with us?"

"Yessir."

"Get O'Brien replaced and released. Set me up on Tach Three."

"Yessir."

144

Hiding Place

I turned to Canelli, just coming down the hallway stairs. "Anything in his room?" I asked.

"Not really. But I . . ."

"We've got to roll. Get into the car. Tune into Tach Three."

"Right." He hurried to the front door. In a few words I relayed O'Brien's information to the Fishers, telling them to remain in the house and await further word.

Twenty-three

Canelli opened the car door for me. "What's all the excitement about, Lieutenant?"

"Just a minute." I picked up the microphone, at the same time gesturing up the block. "Drive to Balboa and turn left. Park at Twenty-seventh."

"Check."

As Canelli drove to the corner and turned left, I requested that a second black-and-white car and an inspector's cruiser be assigned to me, rendezvousing at the Twenty-seventh Avenue corner. Then I instructed that Friedman be advised of the situation.

"Park there," I said. "In the meter."

"Right." Canelli swung the car awkwardly to the curb, setting the brake. Turning in the seat, he sat regarding me with large, hopeful eyes.

With a sigh, I gave him the rundown.

"But I still don't see why all the heat," he said. "I mean, it looks to me like he probably just cut school. Or maybe he ran away to an all-day movie or something."

146

"Why'd you get me out of conference, then, if that's all you thought could've happened?"

He smiled and nodded. "Yeah. I see what you mean."

"I'm beginning to get the feeling," I said, "that the uncle is innocent—and that the kid was telling the truth about Sunday."

"That makes someone else guilty."

"Yes," I said.

"Someone who likes to go around killing kids—two already."

"Yes."

"But the uncle admitted that the boy was lying. You said so yourself, Lieutenant."

"But I didn't find out which day he was lying about. I assumed it was both days. Or, at least, I assumed that he was lying about Sunday, not yesterday. Because the whole case hinges on Sunday, assuming that the two murders are connected."

"Do you think the kid was lying about the dark-haired man yesterday? Is that what you mean?"

"I don't know, Canelli. But assuming the uncle is innocent, then we don't have a looney for a suspect any more. And if we don't have a looney, and it's not a sex crime, then we need a motive. And I'm beginning to think that the motive resulted from some of the little games June Towers was playing. Blackmail, for instance."

He nodded avidly. "And Kent Miller probably knew about it," he said, "and . . ."

The radio crackled to life. "Inspectors Eleven."

I picked up the mike. "Inspectors Eleven," I answered.

"Friedman," came the laconic voice. "Any developments?"

"Negative."

"The boy's still missing?"

"Yes," I answered. "And I'm considering the possibility that his testimony concerning Sunday might have been correct."

"Which makes the mother's statement incorrect."

"Yes. And which also gives us a new suspect, possibly."

A moment of silence. Then: "While you're trying to locate the boy, I'll check out the other possibles."

147

"Roger."

"I'll stay downtown until I find out where we stand. Are you remaining on Tach Three?"

"Yes."

"Roger. Markham and Culligan are on their way to meet you. Out."

As I clicked off the mike, I saw two black-and-white cars converging from opposite ends of the block.

"Tell them to cruise the entire area," I instructed Canelli. "Make sure they're on Tach Three. And find out what else O'Brien knows, if anything. I'm going to take a walk around. You stay with the radio."

"Yessir." Without checking traffic, Canelli swung his driver's door open. A passing Datsun swerved, its horn bleating indignantly. Glancing briefly back at me, Canelli sheepishly raised his shoulders.

I got out on the sidewalk side, standing motionless for a moment, looking down the block toward Twenty-sixth Avenue. It was a typical neighborhood shopping district: grocery stores and liquor stores, a dry-cleaning shop, a beauty shop, a nursery, a hardware store, and a small gas station. At two o'clock on a cold January Wednesday afternoon, threatening rain, there was little activity on Balboa Street. In the entire block, only a dozen cars were parked at the meters.

It was almost directly across the street that O'Brien had apparently first seen the Fisher boy. Living on Twenty-fifth Avenue, between Fulton and Balboa, the boy had been approximately two and a half blocks from home when he was first spotted. He'd been seen about twenty minutes ago, walking. He'd left his home about 8:00 A.M., riding a red bike. O'Brien had seen him about 1:40 P.M.

What had the boy been doing for those five and a half hours?

Where was the bike?

Where was the boy?

And at that moment, where were the other possible suspects?

I walked to the nursery, across the street. A bluff, beefy clerk informed me that he'd been working in the storeroom since

148

lunch, on inventory, and hadn't been able to see the street. I was the first person to come into the store since lunch, he added acidly—not counting a novelty salesman, who'd also taken him away from his inventory count.

I thanked him and went on to the beauty shop and the liquor store, fruitlessly. The time was 2:10. I watched Markham and Culligan cruise by, passing Canelli with hardly a nod. They'd gotten their instructions by radio.

Sample's Superette Market occupied the southeast corner of Twenty-sixth and Balboa. A tall, scrawny youth with half-long hair, a sparse sandy mustache, and pale, discouraged eyes lounged behind the single cash register. His white grocer's smock was wrinkled and stained; his hollow-cheeked face was acne-scarred. Probably deciding that I was a salesman, he eyed me with long-suffering indifference, sucking his teeth loudly.

When I showed him the shield, he came to a kind of slack, shambling attention.

I described David Fisher, stressing the yellow jacket and rust-colored hair, mentioning the possibility of a red five-speed bike.

"Well, I don't know about the bike," he said, "but I think I saw the kid."

"Did he come in the store?"

"No, he stayed outside, on the sidewalk." The clerk pointed through the plate-glass window. "He seemed to be acting kind of suspiciously. That's how I happened to notice him."

"Suspiciously?"

"Yeah. He was hanging around by the mailbox and the telephone pole there. He acted like he was playing cops and robbers, or something." Hearing himself say it, he glanced at me uncertainly, flushing faintly.

"How do you mean?"

"Well, it seemed like he was spying on someone. Or at least it seemed like that to me."

"Could you see who it was that he was spying on?"

"Nope. But I figured it must've been someone in here, because that's where he was looking. In here."

"What time was it?"

149

"Well—" He reflected leisurely, running a forefinger across his upper lip, preening the scraggly mustache. "It must've been about one-thirty. Or maybe a little after. I wasn't keeping track."

"Who was here besides you?"

"Just me. Mr. Sample was still out to lunch. And so was Mrs. Sample," he added pettishly.

"What about customers?"

"I guess there were maybe two, three customers in the store at the time," he answered airily. "I don't remember."

I stepped closer to him, lowering my voice. "I don't know whether you caught my name and rank," I said softly, "but it's Lieutenant Hastings. And this isn't just a 'routine check,' as they say in the movies. This could be very important." I held his eye, silently intimidating him. "Do you understand?"

His prominent Adam's apple bobbed once—then once more. "Y—yes. Yessir. I understand."

"All right. I want you to think about it, and tell me who was in this store while that boy was outside."

He licked his lips as his eyes wandered out toward the sidewalk, then back into the store, scanning the cramped, cluttered shelves. Frowning, he was still stroking his mustache, deep in thought. But finally, he shook his head. "I—it's no use," he said. "I can't think."

I said harshly, "Which way did the boy go when he left? Do you remember that?"

He moved his head toward Twenty-seventh Avenue. "He went that way."

"Are you sure? The boy lives on Balboa."

"I'm sure. He went toward Twenty-seventh Avenue. I remember, because—" He stopped abruptly, eyes slowly widening, mouth slightly agape.

"What is it?" I prompted.

"Well," he said slowly, "I was just going to say that I remember which way the kid went because he went the same way as a customer did. And I remember thinking it was strange that the customer went that way. Because he lives on Twenty-sixth

150

Avenue. And he usually just comes in and then goes right home."

"Do you know the customer's name?"

"Yeah. It's Cross. Mr. Cross."

I drew a deep breath. "Would you say that the boy could have been following Walter Cross?"

The youth brightened. "Hey, yeah. He could've, at that."

I thanked him and stepped out into the street, waving for Canelli to pick me up.

"Go to Walter Cross's house," I said, reaching for the mike, calling Inspectors Twenty-three, Markham's car.

"Inspectors Twenty-three," came the prompt acknowledgment.

"What's your position?" I asked.

"Fulton and Twenty-ninth, proceeding west."

"Seen anything?"

"Negative."

"Have you got a walkie-talkie?"

"Yes."

"All right. Look for us on Twenty-sixth Avenue, about halfway between Fulton and Balboa, on the west side of the street. That's the Cross residence. We'll be parked directly in front of his house. When you see us and spot the house, I want you to drive around in the alley and cover the rear. When you're ready, use your walkie-talkie to advise us. Channel Two. Understood?"

"Understood."

Canelli had already pulled up in front of the Cross residence. The house looked precisely as it had when I'd first seen it: deserted, decaying. Nothing stirred, inside the house or out.

"Is Cross our boy?" Canelli asked.

"Could be. It looks like David was following him. Maybe Cross spotted the boy." I nodded toward the house. "I don't really think that Cross is inside. But we have to check."

"I bet Cross was screwing June Towers. And she started to put the arm on him."

"Maybe," I murmured. I was thinking of my last interview

151

with Cross, and of his sharp, sudden concern when I'd mentioned the possibility of interviewing his stepdaughter, who was still out of town.

Had he been frightened?

Frightened of what?

As I was considering the point, Markham and Culligan cruised by impassively. Waiting for Markham to take up his position, I got on the radio to Friedman, outlining the new situation. He volunteered to coordinate a wider, more intensive search, alerting the park detail and assigning additional units to me on Tach Three. I agreed. As I finished speaking, Markham called in. He was in the alley, ready.

"Let's hit it," I said. "Take the walkie-talkie, Canelli. We can—"

"Inspectors Eleven." It was the radio. "This is O'Brien, Lieutenant."

"What is it, O'Brien?"

"We have a report of the boy entering Golden Gate Park at Thirtieth Avenue, just about a half-hour ago—approximately two P.M."

"Was he walking or riding his bike?"

"Walking."

"Did he appear to be following anyone?"

"I don't know, sir. We got the report from a news vendor. I'll check with him and see whether—"

"Never mind. Proceed to the park. Communications, are you monitoring?"

"Yessir," came Manley's voice.

"Let's get that area covered. We'll be there in five minutes, unless you hear otherwise. We're now at the Cross residence, at"—I glanced at the address—"at 761 Twenty-sixth Avenue. Clear."

"Clear," he acknowledged.

As we approached Cross's front door, Canelli asked, "Are we going inside, Lieutenant?"

"Let's see how the lock looks," I answered shortly. Canelli hadn't yet learned not to comment on occasional illegalities.

152

Hiding Place

While Canelli repeatedly rang the doorbell, I probed the lock with a plastic card, unsuccessfully. "Ask Markham if he can get in the back door," I said. "Hurry it up."

Hunching over the walkie-talkie, Canelli relayed the instructions to Markham. We waited two full minutes. Then, startling me, the latch clicked in my face. The door swung inward. Typically, Markham hadn't kept me advised of his progress.

"No one here," Markham said. "Unless he's hiding."

I took a moment to scan the living room. The place looked exactly as I'd first seen it. I was conscious of a stale, decaying odor—not the strong, unmistakable odor of death, but the subtler scent of neglect and despair.

I turned to Markham. "The kid's been spotted on Fulton and Thirtieth, entering the park, about a half-hour ago. I want you and Culligan to stake this place out, front and back. Get your car out of sight and stay out of sight yourself. He could come back here any time." Without waiting for a reply, I turned abruptly away and took Canelli back to the cruiser.

Twenty-four

I checked the time. "It's two-forty. It's been an hour since he was seen at the grocery store and a half-hour, at least, since he was spotted entering the park." I scanned Fulton Street, where we'd parked. "We're too damn far behind him." I said irritably, "By now he could be a mile away, going in any direction."

"Do you want to cruise around?"

"No. We've got plenty of manpower. What we need now is a break."

"I guess you're right." Canelli was absently shaking the walkie-talkie, banging it against his knee. "We're only about five blocks from the Cross place," he said, "but I can't get Markham on this. These damn things are just about as temperamental as—as"—he frowned—"as anything."

"Hitting it won't do any good."

"A radio repairman told me once that it *did* do some good, though."

"If there're tubes, it's possible. The right vibration can fuse a broken filament inside the tube. But walkie-talkies have transistors."

154

"Oh." He looked at the radio with new vexation. "Well, maybe that's the reason that . . ."

"Inspectors Eleven."

I flipped the switch, acknowledging the call.

"This is Inspectors Fourteen." It was Sigler and Pass. "We're located on a bridle path just south of the intersection of Thirty-fourth Avenue and Fulton. The path is about three hundred feet inside the park, running parallel to Fulton. We've found the boy's yellow jacket. It's got his name in it."

"We'll be right there."

As Canelli got under way, I instructed all units to form a half-mile semicircle around the location of the jacket, with Fulton Street, the park's northern boundary, as the diameter of the half-circle. By the time I'd advised Friedman of the situation, we'd already arrived at Thirty-fourth and Fulton.

"I want you to get four additional units stationed along Fulton," I told Canelli. "Then I want you to stay in the car. If you want me on the walkie-talkie, use Channel Two."

"Yessir." Canelli reached for the microphone as I got out of the cruiser. Inside the park, across a clearing, I saw Sigler waving. As I walked toward him, I surveyed the rough, forest-like terrain. If a fugitive were well concealed, and didn't panic, he could remain hidden here for days.

As I approached, Sigler turned, leading the way through a line of thick-growing cypress and sycamore. Two uniformed men stood looking down at the boy's jacket, lying partially concealed approximately eight feet from the bridle path. As I stooped to examine the jacket, studying the duff-littered ground, I was waywardly wondering whether an Indian scout from a "B" Western could lead us from the jacket to the boy. Certainly none of us could do it. And glancing around the area, I surrendered to a feeling of blind, bitter frustration. Less than a half-hour ago the boy had been here.

"Has anyone tried yelling for him?" I asked suddenly.

Sigler and Pass looked at each other, then shrugged.

"Have you got a walkie-talkie?"

Sigler nodded.

"Then tell everyone to yell for him. His name is David. Let's tell him to come out—that we're police and he's safe."

A moment later the forest-in-the-city was echoing with our shouts, urging the boy to show himself, reassuring him. It was a grim, ominous-sounding parody of childhood hide-and-seek, offering safe passage back to base.

"That's enough," I ordered. "Let's listen."

Sigler relayed the order. We waited, silent.

There was no response. We were rapidly collecting a crowd of rubberneckers. I detailed two men to keep back the curious.

"Give it two more minutes," I told Sigler. "Then have everyone converge on this point, searching. And I *mean* searching. Tell them to look behind every bush and every leaf. The kid could be—" I hesitated. "He could be injured." I stood for a moment irresolutely. Then I decided to return to the car.

Canelli opened the door for me.

"Anything?" I asked, sliding into the seat.

"Afraid not, Lieutenant. I've got three units here on Fulton, besides us."

"I said *four* units."

"Gee, I'm sorry, Lieutenant. I thought you meant . . ."

"Never mind," I said shortly, looking up and down the four-lane thoroughfare. The time was exactly 2:50 P.M. Almost two hours had passed since the boy had been reported missing.

Had Cross been the dark-haired man in the white Ford?

Had the boy found him today—followed him?

Had Cross seen David and led him down Balboa Street, away from the Fisher neighborhood, luring him finally into the park?

Had the mother lied, not the boy? Had she . . .

"Inspectors Eleven." It was Friedman's voice.

I clicked the mike to "transmit." "Inspectors Eleven."

"Any developments?"

"I'm having the area searched, converging on the boy's jacket."

"How's the terrain?"

"Terrible."

156

"I was afraid of that. Do you want me to come out there?"

"Not until we get a line on the suspect," I replied. "He could be anywhere."

"Is the suspect on foot?"

"As far as I know."

"He might still be in the park, or making for home. Have you got his house staked out?"

"Of course," I answered, irritated. "Front and back. Culligan and Markham."

"How are the kid's parents taking it?"

"Not very well."

I heard him draw a deep breath. "The uncle," he said slowly, "is just staring at the wall. I can't get a peep out of him. Even when I told him that David was missing, he didn't respond."

I realized that I was again experiencing the same sense of dull, inarticulate outrage I'd first felt Monday, interviewing the uncle and the boy. And finally I recognized the source of that irritation: the man and the boy were losers, both of them. They were first- and second-generation victim-types, the grist of a cop's eight-hour day. All his life James had been beaten on. Now it was David's turn. He could . . .

". . . you hear me?" Friedman was asking.

"Yes. Sorry." I took a moment to collect myself. I suddenly realized that I was bone-tired. "I'd better check with Sigler, in the park. I'll get back to you."

As Friedman went off the air, I got Sigler on the walkie-talkie. He had nothing to report. They'd found no sign of either Cross or the boy. The search was finished, Sigler said. Everyone was standing around the area where the jacket had been found, awaiting instructions. I ordered six units to cruise the park again, leaving Sigler, Pass, and four uniformed men in the vicinity of the jacket.

Beside me, Canelli was yawning, looking at his watch. "Maybe the kid just dropped his jacket," he offered. "That's what happens with kids. I remember my mother always used to say that—"

"Inspectors Eleven." It was the car radio—Tach Three.

157

"Go ahead," I replied, recognizing the voice as Culligan's. "I'm in front of the Cross house," Culligan said, "in the car. And I've just heard from Sergeant Markham, in the backyard." Culligan's voice was low, involuntarily tensed. "He says the suspect has just turned into the alley behind the house. The suspect is walking north from Fulton, approximately three hundred feet from the house."

Signaling for Canelli to get under way fast, I said, "We're approximately seven blocks from you, proceeding east on Fulton, heading for the entrance to the alley. Are your walkie-talkies on Channel Two?"

"Yessir."

"We'll be there in approximately two minutes." And addressing the six units cruising the park, I quickly outlined the situation, then said, "I want three units on Twenty-seventh Avenue between Fulton and Balboa, and the other three units on Twenty-sixth. Spread out, so the suspect is bottled up in the block he's in now. But don't move in on him, and stay away from the entrances to the alley. Code Two—no sirens. I don't want the suspect spooked. I don't think he's armed, but I'm not sure. So use caution. Out." I picked up the walkie-talkie. "Can you hear me, Markham?"

"Roger." His voice came through indistinctly.

"What's it look like?"

"He's about two hundred feet away. He's walking slowly, looking around. But he isn't stopping. He's acting suspiciously."

"You might have to take him, Markham," I said quietly. "We might not make it in time. I want you to go slow and easy. I don't think he's armed. If you can, prevent him from getting inside the house. And whatever you do, don't shoot unless it's absolutely necessary. We still haven't found the boy. If Cross can't talk, we might never find him."

"I'll take Cross in the yard," came Markham's voice, tenser now. "I'm concealed behind some shrubbery, so I should be able to surprise him. It won't be long now. Out."

158

Canelli was swinging across the traffic, making for the alley's entrance.

"Park on Fulton," I said hastily. "Don't go into the alley. I don't want him to see us."

As he swung into a nearby driveway, I got out of the car, loosening my pistol. Gesturing for Canelli to stay behind me, I peered around the stucco corner of a garage.

I could clearly see Cross's back. He was walking slowly—plainly tense, wary. Now he was hesitating, standing in the alleyway's center, beginning to turn back toward us, pivoting slowly. With only half my face exposed, I didn't move, confident that he couldn't see me. His right hand was thrust into the pocket of his sports jacket. Did he have a gun? He was almost facing his own backyard, half turned away from us.

"Okay," I whispered. "You go along the far side of the alley."

"Right," Canelli breathed, easing around me. He held the walkie-talkie in his left hand, his gun in the other.

Moving slowly, taking advantage of every opportunity for cover, we advanced cautiously. From behind me, I heard the low, excited sound of children's voices. I regretted not ordering the men still in the park to guard the alley entrances. I should have . . .

Suddenly Cross turned toward us, full face. He looked first at Canelli, then at me. With guns drawn, our purpose was plain. For an instant all motion ceased; the suspect seemed suspended, jerked up by some invisible thread, then frozen in a grotesquely fragmented pirouette.

"Hold it right there, Cross," I called, stepping into the middle of the alley. "Don't move."

The sound of my voice convulsed him into a spasm of wild, violent movement. As his head jerked toward Markham, on his left, Cross's right hand came out of his pocket. I crouched, raising my revolver, aiming.

The hand was empty. Both hands, in plain view, were empty. "Okay," I shouted. "Let's take him. Let's . . ."

Cross backed away, moving as if he were hypnotized. Mark-

159

ham was slowly advancing on him, pistol ready. Cross raised his right hand to Markham, gesturing in hesitant, begging protest, warding Markham off.

Then, as Canelli and I began to trot toward him, Cross whirled, heedless of Markham's gun, making for a wooden fence, clambering quickly over, gone. Canelli immediately stopped running, raising his walkie-talkie.

"He's in a backyard on Twenty-seventh Avenue," Canelli said loudly. "About halfway up the block. He could be breaking out."

Sprinting toward the wooden fence, I called over my shoulder, "Tell them he's unarmed, Canelli. No shooting."

Ahead of me, running across the alley, Markham first rattled a locked gate, then scaled the fence. Beyond him, I saw Cross scrabbling over a second fence, making for another backyard. Behind me, I heard Canelli excitedly shouting into the walkie-talkie. Culligan was running toward us, his topcoat flapping as he ran, all awkward arms and legs.

"He's in that yard, Culligan," I shouted, pointing. "The one with the high fence." Holstering my gun, I scaled the same fence Cross and Markham had climbed. As I went over, I saw Markham pulling himself to the top of the higher fence. I saw him hesitate. Now he was sitting on top of the redwood fence, one leg over, the other dangling on my side. It was at least six feet high—higher than I'd first thought.

Panting, I was beside Markham now, drawing my gun to cover him. But Markham remained motionless. He was staring into the neighboring yard. His gun was holstered. He . . .

A woman screamed. Immediately another voice joined the first—two women, screaming. Now a child's cry sounded, terrified.

On tiptoe, drawing myself up, I looked over the fence. Cross was sitting sprawled in a child's sandbox. With one arm he clutched a squirming tow-headed little girl close to his body. With the other hand he held a child's small metal sandbox shovel. Cross gripped the shovel like a hand ax, drawn back, aimed at the child's head. Suddenly the fence was ringed with

160

bobbing heads—uniform hats, felt hats, bare heads—all of them popping up and dropping back as strained arm muscles failed.

"Go away," Cross screamed. "Go away or I'll kill her." As he said it I saw the child wince. Her head was pressed tight against Cross's chest; her long blond hair covered one of his shoulders. She was a preschool child, three or four years old.

Behind me, Canelli was swearing softly. From inside the house next door, a woman was screaming "Jeannie" over and over.

"Get down from there, Markham," I said. And to Canelli: "Give me a leg up. Then go to the car. Call Friedman. Get a sharpshooter. Tell Friedman to come with the sharpshooter."

"Yessir. Here, how's this?" He knelt, offering his pudgy thigh.

"Good. Thanks." As Markham lowered himself, I stepped up on Canelli's knee and pulled myself to the top of the fence, then dropped down on the other side, moving cautiously, watching Cross constantly. His eyes followed every movement. If I went for him—startled him—he'd bring the sharp metal shovel slashing down into the little girl's skull.

I stood motionless, my empty hands limp at my sides. For a long, silent moment Cross stared at me. The child's head obscured the lower half of his face, revealing only the dark, smoldering eyes.

"Let her go, Cross," I said quietly. "You've got enough trouble without this."

"Bring a car, Lieutenant. Bring a car and park it in the alley. I'm driving out of here." His voice was low, choked. His eyes were ominously steady. He meant it, every word.

"You're *walking* out of here, Cross. With us."

He suddenly giggled in a high, hysterical falsetto.

"Put the shovel down," I said, "and get to your . . ."

From my left, I caught a flash of movement. With an open door swinging wide behind her, a woman in a red-checkered apron flung herself into the backyard, running wildly. She stumbled, falling headlong on a flagstone patio, hitting hard.

"My baby," she was screaming. "Give me my baby."

"*Hold it.*" I moved quickly toward her, keeping my distance from Cross. But before I could reach her, the woman was on her feet. Her palms were bloody, and one knee.

"Let him alone," I said. "Let us handle it. Get back in the house." I saw Cross standing erect, the shovel raised against the woman. With Cross's arm clamped across her chest, the child dangled clear of the ground, legs helplessly twitching. She was whimpering.

As I moved to get between them, I saw the woman lunge. Teeth bared, fingers talon-crooked, she was screaming incoherently. Cross fell back a single step. The shovel was raised higher now—poised, ready.

"Cross," I was yelling, gathering myself. "Don't be a . . ."

The woman was on him. The shovel flashed up, then down. I was hurling myself forward, leaving my feet. The shovel came up again. Twisting as I struck the surging tangle of limbs and bodies, I grabbed for the shovel, finding it with my fingertips, gripping it hard. The woman was beneath me. She faced the sky, screaming. Blood flecked her forehead. Momentarily our faces touched. Then, still holding the handle, I rolled free, throwing my full body's weight against the shovel, feeling it rip from his hand. Looking up, I saw blue-uniformed legs and flailing blue arms. I saw a fist crash into the side of Cross's face and realized that I was clutching him by the hair. I felt him go slack.

"That's enough," I panted. "No more."

On my knees, still holding the shovel, struggling for breath, I looked closely at the woman and child, wailing in each other's arms. The woman's scalp wounds seemed slight, even though blood flowed into her hair and down her forehead. She wasn't stunned; her eyes were clear.

"Mommy, Mommy," the girl was crying. Just the one word, constantly.

With three uniformed men holding him spread-eagled beside the sandbox, Cross glared up at me. He didn't move—didn't twitch, didn't struggle.

"Where is he, Cross?" I asked. "Where's David Fisher?"

162

Unwavering, he didn't reply.

Still gripping the shovel, I said, "Where is he, you degenerate sonofabitch? Tell me, or I'll tear your eyes out of your head —with this." I held the shovel hard against his cheek, an inch from his eye.

He laughed at me. It was an animal sound, deep in his throat. He hardly blinked—didn't wince. "That would be against the law, Lieutenant."

I moved the shovel, placing the blade a precisely calculated half-inch below his right eye. Blood smeared his cheek. It was the woman's blood. "No one will ever know, Cross," I whispered. "It could have happened while we were fighting."

Breath rattling, he didn't speak. He wasn't afraid. I stared down at him for another long, malevolent moment, then got to my feet. I turned to Markham and gave him the shovel. I stepped away from the group clustered around Cross, motioning for Markham to follow me. "I want you to get him in your car and take him to Fulton and Thirty-second Avenue, near where Sigler found the kid's jacket."

"But we're supposed to take him . . ."

"Never mind. This won't take long. In an hour and a half, with these clouds, it'll be dark. I'm going to find that kid."

"But the kid could be dead."

"Then we'll find his body. I'm going to my car. I'll see you at Fulton and Thirty-second. Let's move it." I turned abruptly away, ignoring his rule-book protests.

Twenty-five

As I slid into the cruiser I felt Canelli's eyes on me.

"How'd it go?" he asked, glancing at my disheveled clothing.

"No problem. But he won't tell us where the kid is." I lay back against the seat, eyes closed, and surrendered to the sudden ache of a deep, despairing fatigue. "Drive to Fulton and Thirty-second," I muttered. "Anything on the radio?"

"No. I canceled the sharpshooter."

"Good. Is Friedman coming?"

"Not now. He said he'd wait to hear from you. He said that—"

"Inspectors Eleven."

Wearily I acknowledged the call.

"This is Sigler, Lieutenant. Is everything all right?"

"If we can find the boy, it'll be all right."

He paused briefly. Then: "We just found something that looks like it could've been used for a club, Lieutenant." I could hear a note of regret in his voice. "It's a branch, about two inches in diameter, twenty-four inches long. It's, ah—" Again he paused. "It's got fresh blood on it. I don't think the blood's more than an hour old."

164

Hiding Place

As Canelli was muttering "sonofabitch" I heard myself breathing a string of obscenities. I was thinking that a cop's business is blood. He's an expert at judging its age and its significance, and its probable origins within the body.

"How far is the club from the jacket?" I asked.

"About a quarter of a mile, I'd say."

"Is the terrain rugged?"

"Yessir."

"Well," I said slowly, "the only thing we can do is start another search, with the club as a center. We'll use everyone who's here. We're bringing the suspect, too."

"The suspect?" Sigler was plainly surprised.

"Yes," I answered firmly, "the suspect. We'll be there in a few minutes. All of us. I'll give the necessary orders."

"Yessir."

I beckoned to Markham and Culligan, standing on either side of the handcuffed prisoner. Culligan was a tall, angular man with a sallow complexion, a duodenal ulcer, and a nagging wife. As he prodded Cross forward, Culligan looked more than usually unhappy.

"Bring him over here," I ordered. And to the four policemen assigned to crowd control: "I want everyone back. Even the reporters. I'll talk to them later."

"Yessir."

As Markham came within a few paces of me, he said in a low voice, "I want you to know that I'm doing this under protest, Lieutenant. The regulations—the law—states that a suspect is to be taken directly to the appropriate station house and charged."

I turned to Culligan, who'd been listening covertly, eyes averted. "You're his witness, Culligan. I'll expect you to so testify."

Culligan's sad, hollow eyes, sunk deep into a long, gaunt face, were expressionless. Almost imperceptibly he shrugged, still looking away.

"Bring Cross over there," I ordered, "behind those trees." And to Canelli I said, "Get the walkie-talkie, will you? And get

165

set up with someone in a car so that you're in touch with Communications. Then catch up with us. I want you to stick with me."

I led the way behind a thick-growing screen of trees. The bridle path was just ahead—and the boy's yellow jacket, still lying where we'd first found it. I stopped beside the jacket, turning to face Cross.

The suspect stood quietly, his pale face rigid. Now his mouth twitched slightly, as if he were suppressing some subtle, secret joke.

I decided on an oblique opening, hopefully to catch him off balance. "We've just interviewed your stepdaughter, Cross," I said quietly. "While you were running—threatening to kill that little girl—we were interrogating your stepdaughter." I paused, watching him closely. "How does that make you feel?"

His sardonic eyes didn't answer, his mouth remained steady, composed. He moved his head toward Markham. "You'd better listen to him, Lieutenant. When my lawyer hears that you've been . . ."

I realized that I'd stepped close to him, was whispering furiously, "I want to know where the boy is, Cross. I figure that you picked up a stick and beat that kid until he's bloody. Maybe you killed him. And if you did kill him, then I want to know where the body is. And if . . ." I deliberately turned, pointing to a nearby cluster of thick, high laurel. "And if you won't tell me about it right now—right here—I'll take you behind those bushes and I'll beat you till you bleed inside." I paused, still with my face barely a foot from his, still whispering, half choked by my own boiling fury.

"Do you understand, Cross?" I finally asked, my voice still hoarse.

He didn't answer. Looking me directly in the eye, he seemed no more than an indifferent spectator, watching me as I fumed helplessly.

"You killed June Towers because of what she knew about you," I said softly. "And you probably killed Kent Miller for the same reason. But the boy—ten years old—" I stopped, suppressing a sudden desire to crash my fist into his simpering, supercilious face.

He'd never tell me. Not now. Not here. I was wasting time—and daylight.

I turned away from him, saying, "Get him out of here, Markham. Take him downtown. Interrogate him for the record, and book him."

I heard them leaving, walking noisily through the underbrush. I heard Markham say something, and heard Cross answer. In the distance, I heard the sounds and the shouts of my men, searching.

The boy was dead. I could sense it—feel it. I could clearly visualize the battered, bludgeoned body.

A pine bough, cone-laden, hung close to my face. Suddenly I was balling my fist, striking the closest cone, sending it flying. My knuckles stung. Looking down, I saw blood flecks on my hand. "An interior decorator," I said softly. "A goddamn interior decorator."

Canelli had come to stand beside me, patiently waiting for my anger to subside. In the two years I'd known him, I'd never once seen Canelli angry.

Exhaling slowly, I glanced at my watch, then looked up into the sky. "We'd better arrange for searchlights," I said finally. "In another hour it'll be dark."

"Yessir." Canelli lifted the walkie-talkie, relaying my instructions. Then, for a long, futile half-minute we stood side by side, avoiding each other's glance, staring silently at the thick-growing trees, listening to the muffled shouts of the searchers.

They could come across him at any moment. Dead leaves would cover the body; mud would be mixed with the drying blood.

Or, instead, some wayward stroller would someday stumble on a hand, or a foot, perhaps first unearthed by marauding dogs. Sometimes the exposed limbs were found half eaten. Sometimes . . .

"It's too bad we can't find some of the kids he plays with,"

Canelli was saying. "He might have some kind of a secret place, or something, where he's hiding."

At first I heard him only dimly. But in the next moment I turned on him, grabbing his arm. "Call in to Friedman," I said. "Tell him to bring the uncle out here. Fast."

He frowned. "The uncle?"

"The uncle." I shook the beefy forearm. "Hurry up, Canelli. Put in the goddamn call. Tell Friedman I'm expecting him in fifteen minutes."

Twenty-six

Impatiently, I glanced at my watch. The time was precisely four o'clock. It had been almost ten minutes since Canelli had called Friedman. We'd taken up a position behind the first fringe of trees, allowing us to observe the crowd clustered on Fulton Street. Canelli had propped the walkie-talkie in the crotch of a huge pine tree—a "good climbing tree," the kids would call it. Would Canelli forget the walkie-talkie? Should I . . .

A blue sedan was erratically angling across Fulton, pulling to a stop behind a police station wagon. Marge and Bill Fisher got out of the blue sedan, heedlessly leaving the door open. Both were gesturing furiously, confronting Sigler. I saw Canelli watching the Fishers. He was clicking his teeth, registering a wry distaste.

"Tell Sigler to let them come up here," I said briefly.

Looking at me with mild puzzlement, Canelli reached for the walkie-talkie and contacted Sigler.

"Maybe you'd better put that in your pocket," I said, gesturing to the walkie-talkie.

"Oh. Yeah."

We watched the Fishers approaching. The man was ten feet

169

ahead of the woman, who was laboring over the uneven terrain in pink plastic playshoes. It was a slight uphill grade, and Fisher was breathing hard as he reached me, saying, "Where is he? Is he all right? Is he . . ." He paused, gulping for air. His wife pulled up at his side, panting.

"We haven't found him yet," I answered shortly. "Do you have any idea where we could look, Mr. Fisher?"

Scanning the silent trees with a baffled, baleful stare, Fisher shook his head sharply. He stood with his big fists bunched at his sides, his bullet head lowered on his thick neck, chin outthrust. He looked like a prizefighter awaiting the bell.

"Do *you* have any ideas, Mrs. Fisher?"

Ignoring the question, she was looking back the way they'd come, momentarily oblivious of me. "What's *he* doing here?" she whispered.

Following her line of sight, I saw Friedman and James Fisher walking slowly toward us. Friedman's head was down as he trudged doggedly up the grade. Fisher was walking easily, his blank stare focused straight ahead, unmindful of the rough ground.

"What's he *doing* here?" Repeating the question, her voice was very low, barely audible. "Why isn't he handcuffed?"

She didn't know about Cross, then. She'd learned of our search for David, concentrating in the park. But she hadn't heard about Cross, or about his capture. She still thought David had simply run away. She didn't realize that her son might have been injured—or killed.

"James is innocent, Mrs. Fisher. He was innocent all the time." I paused, turning to assess her reaction as I said, "You knew that, didn't you? Even when you were contradicting David's story—even when you were phoning in the tip to us—you knew James was innocent."

Her eyes were fierce as she twisted to face me. Her fingers were claw-crooked, involuntarily half raised against me. "You're a liar—a dirty liar."

Out of the corner of my eye I glimpsed Bill Fisher turning to look at his wife. I could sense the force of the husband's dull,

170

incredulous outrage as I said, "You obstructed justice, Mrs. Fisher. You . . ."

"He *was* in the park when the girl was killed," she flared. "That's all I said. That's all I . . ."

"But you had no reason to think David lied. And in fact *you* lied, suggesting that David and James weren't together all the time on Sunday. So when you led us to believe that David hadn't told the truth, you were—"

"You phoned the police?" Fisher's voice was ominously low. "*You?*"

She swung on him, her hands twitching. "You're away all day. You don't know what it's like, locked up with a maniac. You don't *care*. You don't know what people think—what they say. You just—just—" Her mouth was working furiously as she glared at her husband, finally forcing him to drop his eyes, defeated. As Friedman and James Fisher joined us, the woman turned to face her brother-in-law. But her rage-choked words were meant for her husband as she said, "If he comes back in that house, I'll leave. I swear to God, I'll leave." Her voice vibrated with a venomous, low-pitched sibilance. She took a single quick, threatening step toward James. Friedman stepped forward to ward her off, raising a beefy hand.

Bill Fisher gazed first at his wife, then at his brother. As he began to speak, Bill seemed dazed. "You're talking about what people think?" he said dully.

She whirled, rounding on him, her eyes blazing. "That's right," she whispered. "That's right—that's what I'm telling you. I'm *sick* of it. I'm sick of him. I'm . . ." Whatever she was going to say was lost in a sudden sob and her eyes glazed with angry tears. Then, wheeling blindly, she started to run down toward the cars, stumbling, half falling.

Her husband stood quietly, gazing after her. "That's all she cares about," he said finally. "That house. Lately, whenever she's getting ready for company, it's like— Well, I can't do anything around that goddamn house. It—it's like it didn't even belong to me any more." Mutely he looked at each of us in turn, as though seeking something from us. Finally his eyes settled on his brother. The two men looked at each other sadly. Then, turning slowly away, moving heavily, Fisher followed his wife down the slope.

James Fisher's dark, inscrutable eyes were utterly calm—dead calm.

Could I reach him with mere words, spark those dead eyes into life?

Speaking very slowly, trying to compel his attention, I explained what had happened in the past few hours, beginning with the proof of his own innocence, ending with our discovery of the bloody club. I pointed up into the sky, explaining that it would soon be dark and rainy. If we didn't find David soon, I said, the boy could be out all night in the rain, injured.

As I finished speaking, I saw Friedman glance at his watch. The time, I knew, must be well after four. Visibility was lessening by the minute.

I saw James Fisher's lips stir.

Was he struggling to reply?

Could he reply?

The lusterless, lifeless eyes gave no clue. The pale face was frozen, catatonic. Only the lips moved, struggling with some half-formed thought. Finally he managed a single word: "Rain?" As he said it, the dark brows drew together. "Will David be—wet?"

"Yes, Mr. Fisher. If we don't find him soon—if we can't help him, he'll get wet. He could lie all night in the rain. And right now he could be injured—badly injured."

He stared at me for a long moment, maddeningly deliberate. Then, turning his whole body, he stared at Friedman questioningly.

Friedman nodded solemnly. "That's right," he said softly. "He'll get wet. And we're almost certain he's hurt."

Another moment passed. Then, oblivious of the three of us, Fisher turned woodenly away, walking stiffly, his dead eyes staring straight ahead. He was striding parallel to the bridle path, moving in the opposite direction from the yellow jacket and the bloodied tree limb.

172

"Have someone bring us a couple of lights," I whispered to Canelli.

He fell back, relaying the order in a low voice, using the walkie-talkie. Friedman and I followed Fisher, letting him go ahead. Now he was angling away from the path, climbing a low ridge, thickly overgrown.

"Was this area searched?" Friedman asked softly, breathing heavily.

"I don't think so."

"I hope he knows what he's doing. We've got about twenty minutes of daylight, at the outside."

I glanced over my shoulder. Carrying two small searchlights, Canelli was trotting after us, puffing. I put my finger to my lips. Nodding, Canelli slowed to a walk.

"Frank. Look," Friedman was whispering now.

Turning, I saw Fisher standing near a gnarled, big-boled cypress growing at an improbable angle out from the side of the hill. Downhill erosion had exposed a cagelike, tangled cluster of cypress roots. As I watched, Fisher sank to his knees.

"David?" Fisher spoke softly, querulously.

I stepped forward and knelt beside him, and saw a dark cave-cage that went back into the hillside. I beckoned to Canelli, requesting one of the lights.

"David? Are you in there?" Fisher's voice was very low.

There was no answer—no sound of movement.

"Here—" Canelli handed one light to me, the other to Friedman. Kneeling side by side, we switched on the lights.

The boy lay curled in the fetal position, wedged far back in his tiny cave. Blood matted his hair, streaked his face, soaked his shirt front.

I handed my light to Canelli as I stretched out on the ground, reaching to my arm's full length through the twisted roots. My groping fingers fell a foot short of the motionless body.

But with his two-foot club Cross could have reached him. Cross could have . . .

"Let's get some axes up here," Friedman snapped. "And a stretcher. Hurry it up. Call the fire department rescue squad."

173

Hastily Canelli relayed the orders. Friedman held both lights, training them on the boy's face. "He's alive," Friedman said softly. "He's breathing."

"*Just* breathing."

"That could be shock."

"He's lost a lot of blood."

"I don't know," Friedman said critically. "No more than the usual head wound, I'd say. And I don't see any brain tissue."

"Great," I answered dryly, getting my legs under me, rising to face Fisher, also on his feet. "Losing that much blood," I said, "and being in shock—unconscious—he couldn't have gotten through the night, probably. If he lives, you can thank yourself for it."

In the gathering darkness, he nodded gravely, just once. Then he turned back to face the cypress—head bowed, waiting quietly.

Twenty-seven

"What's the doc say?" Canelli slumped beside me on the waiting-room couch, extending his legs full length, crossing his ankles. Canelli invariably wore low-cut black shoes with white sweat socks.

"It's just a concussion," I answered. "The skull isn't fractured."

"Is he conscious?"

"Yes. His parents are with him now. We can talk to him in ten minutes or so."

"Well, *that's* a relief. About the concussion, I mean—and no brain damage."

"We *hope* there's no brain damage."

"Yeah. I— Oh, say, I forgot. Your friend is downstairs. Mrs. Haywood."

"Ann?"

"Yeah. She said to tell you she's waiting dinner for you. But I think she wouldn't mind seeing the kid. She used to teach him, she said." He hesitated, then added, "She's sure nice. She's got real class."

"Go down and get her, will you?" I considered a moment,

finally saying, "Then, if you want to, you can go home. All I need now is a statement from the boy. You can witness it in the morning, if you don't mind taking my word for what he said."

Rising promptly to his feet, he smiled. "Well, I *am* a little hungry. But if you want me to, I can sure stick around, Lieutenant."

"No, never mind. Just tell Mrs. Haywood to come up." I smiled. "I'd rather talk to her than you."

Returning the smile, he waved awkwardly. "Yeah. I see what you mean. Well—" He waved again. "See you tomorrow, Lieutenant."

"Right. And thanks, Canelli."

"That's okay. See you." He turned away, narrowly avoiding a sand-filled ashstand.

Quickly glancing up and down the deserted hallway, I kissed her as she stepped from the elevator. Startled, she first squirmed, then giggled, finally returning the kiss with a sudden, playful lust. Momentarily aroused, I could feel her body secretly, subtly responding to mine.

She stepped back, smiling into my eyes. "Are you on duty, Lieutenant?"

"Just going off. Would you like to go off duty with me?"

"I've got a roast in the oven."

"Let it burn."

"We have to eat, though. We . . ."

Wheeling a stainless-steel lab cart, a nurse was turning a nearby corner. Test tubes tinkled like wind chimes. The nurse smiled at us impersonally.

"Come on—the waiting room's down here." As I fell into step beside Ann, I saw David's door opening. A nurse came out, nodded to me, and turned in the opposite direction. The doctor was still inside with the parents. The doctor had promised the parents fifteen minutes. Then I would have my turn.

Seating herself primly in an easy chair, Ann's eyes darkened as she asked, "How is he?"

"As far as I know, he'll be all right. Still, when anyone's been unconscious for that length of time as a result of a blow on the head, there's always the possibility of brain damage."

She caught her breath. "Oh, no."

I looked down at my lap, examining the knuckles of my clenched right fist.

"How long was he unconscious?"

"About forty-five minutes."

"What kind of a person could have done that—attack a child with a club? It—it's bestial."

I was aware that, to her, I might seem indifferent, yet I could only answer with one short, expressionless phrase: "He was scared."

"The murderer?"

"Yes."

"Is he a pervert?"

"No, I wouldn't say so."

"But what *is* he?" she pressed, her eyes snapping indignantly. "What made him do it?"

I sighed. "I've already told you: he was scared. Literally, he was scared to death. He had a guilty conscience. And guilty consciences catch more criminals than smart cops. Believe me."

She drew a deep, exasperated breath. "Either tell me how it happened, or don't tell me. But please don't tease me, Frank. Don't be cryptic. It—it's unfair. And besides, you're reminding me of your friend Pete Friedman, playing cat-and-mouse."

"If I tell you, you're sure to tell the kids in your class." I was trying to match her half-bantering mood.

"Probably."

"Hmm."

"You're still teasing me." Now there was a hint of vexation in her voice.

I sighed again, saying, "It's very simple, really. Cross murdered his wife, probably by administering a barbiturate overdose. Or maybe he just didn't bother to prevent her from taking an overdose."

"Is that a crime?"

"It depends. But in any case, he was guilty—in his own mind, at least. Apparently it showed, and June picked up on it. Living so close to the Cross family, it's not surprising. So June proceeded to try a little blackmail. She started out on a small scale, as most blackmailers do—twenty bucks here and twenty bucks there. Then it got to be fifty, then a hundred. And as insurance, she told Kent Miller about her little sideline. So—" I spread my hands. "So Walter Cross met June Towers in the park, by prearrangement, and he killed her. He told her that he was going to make a payoff. He planned it carefully. He very cleverly rented a getaway car, which he dutifully returned the next day. And he bludgeoned her to death. To make it look like robbery, he rifled her purse and even stole her car, which took nerve. But he had one more problem."

"What was it?"

"Before she died, June Towers told Cross that Kent Miller knew about the blackmail scheme."

"So Cross killed Kent Miller."

"Yes. And by that time, thanks to Marge Fisher, David's uncle was a suspect. So Cross tried to set up Fisher for both murders, by stealing a so-called murder weapon from the Fishers' potting shed. It was a clumsy attempt. But it probably would've worked if it hadn't been for David."

"David?"

I nodded, obscurely pleased at her rapt, wide-eyed interest. "David cut school today, and he played detective. He'd seen Cross yesterday, just before Cross stole the pruning shears—the fake murder weapon. No one believed David had seen him, least of all David's mother. But he *did* see Cross, and today he went looking for him. Maybe he even knew where Cross lives. We don't know yet. But David found him. And you know the rest."

"Cross would actually have killed him," she said slowly. "I can't believe it. I just can't."

"When he saw David following him," I replied, "he knew that David had 'made him,' as we say. He knew it was just a matter of time before we'd hear about him, from David. Cross was desperate. Thanks to David, his time was running out."

"What about James Fisher? Will he be all right?"

I hesitated, then said, "He's out at the county hospital—in the psychiatric ward, for observation. It's—" Again I hesitated, dropping my eyes. "It's probable that he'll be institutionalized. He just hasn't got any other place to . . ."

With a start I realized that the doctor was standing in the archway. I introduced Ann, explaining that she had been David's teacher.

"I think he'll be all right," the doctor said briskly. "So far, anyhow, so good. No evidence of any trauma."

"Can I question him?"

"For fifteen minutes, no more. His parents are leaving right now. He's sedated, so don't be surprised if he's a little woozy. His mind might seem to wander, too. Otherwise, no problem. We didn't even have to give him any blood. Well—" He offered me a wide, muscular hand. "I've got things to do." Nodding to Ann, running a quick, appreciative eye over her figure, he turned on his heel and walked quickly down the hallway, his white coat billowing behind him, revealing mod-striped trousers.

As the doctor passed David's door, it opened. The Fishers emerged. Before closing the door, the mother looked back into the room. Almost timidly, she waved, then let the door close.

I stood in the waiting-room archway, silently watching them as they walked to the elevator. Beside me, Ann whispered, "Is that them? The parents?"

I nodded, keeping my eyes on the man and wife. As Fisher pressed the "down" button his eyes strayed aside, briefly meeting mine, then falling away. A whispered word passed between the two. Together they raised their heads, staring up at the elevator arrow climbing slowly.

I stepped forward, clearing my throat. Twenty-five feet of white-tiled corridor separated us. Fifteen feet. Ten. The elevator was on the next floor down, ascending.

"How is he?" I asked.

The elevator doors slid noiselessly open. Without looking at me, Marge Fisher stepped into the empty elevator. With a glance of quick, furtive apology, the husband followed. Once inside, the woman turned to face me, her back to the gleaming metal wall of the elevator. Eying me with calm, silent disdain, she reached deliberately forward, arm fully extended, to press the control button. Beside her, Bill Fisher muttered that David was fine—just fine.

As the doors began to slide closed, I raised my hand, touching the black rubber bumper. The doors sprang back. "Do you realize," I said softly, "that David wouldn't even be in that room if it weren't for you?" As I said it I looked directly at the woman. My voice, I realized, shook slightly. "You tried to set up your own brother-in-law for a murder charge. You didn't quite succeed, of course. But you undoubtedly succeeded in robbing James of whatever sanity he had left. Which for your purposes, I suppose, is just as good. But in the process you also succeeded in almost getting your own son killed. Because if you hadn't fingered James, Cross would never have tried to set him up, and David would never have become involved."

I paused a moment, drawing a deep, unsteady breath. "If Cross could have reached a foot farther inside that cave," I said slowly, "you'd have a dead son." Again I paused before finally saying, "I'm not going to ask the D.A. for an indictment against you for obstructing justice, Mrs. Fisher. In the first place, he probably wouldn't comply. And in the second place—more to the point—I wouldn't want to put David through an experience like that—seeing you get what you deserve. I just couldn't cut it."

Tapping my hand on the black rubber bumper, I had the satisfaction of seeing the shame and guilt in her eyes. I allowed the door to half close before I deliberately tapped it open again, this time holding it.

"I'm sure you're going to be spending a lot of time telling your friends what a monster Cross is—how he almost killed your boy. But I'd like you to know, Mrs. Fisher, that while you're telling your friends about Cross, I'm going to be telling the men in the squad room about you. We see bastards like Cross every day—he's our stock in trade. But we don't often see someone like you."

I released the doors. They slid smoothly together.

I turned abruptly away—colliding with Ann. As I hastily

D 13

180

grabbed her arm, steadying her, I saw that her eyes were tear-brimmed.

"That was one hell of a speech, Lieutenant," she whispered. "That was really one hell of a speech."

I cleared my throat, muttering something. Then, still holding her arm, I turned her toward David's room.

About the Author

COLLIN WILCOX was born in Detroit and educated at Antioch College. He's been a San Franciscan since 1949, and lives in a Victorian house that he's "constantly remodeling, with the help of two strong sons." In addition to writing a book a year, Mr. Wilcox designs and manufactures his own line of decorator lamps and wall plaques.